Yvonne,

I hope
you enjoy!

Christmas Lights

(A Small Town Romance)

By

Liberty Blake

This book is dedicated to Hannah Howell and the members of the Maine Chapter (MERWA). Every spring I look forward to going to Maine with Hannah for the writers retreat. I have met fabulous people at the retreat and I love each and every one of you.

Thank you for being gracious hostesses and wonderful friends.

~~~~~~~Thank you~~~~~~~
Skye and Amanda,
You are the best of editors,
Fearless taskmasters,
And inspirations

Thank you to Jillian for everything.

And as always, thank you to my Crazy Crew (Karen Frisch, Maeve Christopher, JM Griffin, Dana Stone, & in spirit Janet Jones). Without our business brunches I would be lost.

Chapter 1

"All aboard." The conductor's voice rang inside the confines of the passenger car, bouncing from the locomotive and the brick station building and back. Azure Brown smiled at the clouds of steam issuing from the man's mouth as his warm breath met the cold air. Snow covered his wool clad shoulders and his company hat was almost as white as his hair.

"I wanna go home." The strident voice of a toddler drew Azzie's attention from her quiet contemplation of the weather toward a gorgeous hunk carrying a toddler who was obviously out past her bedtime.

Azzie had thought she was immune to good looking men. She saw them all the time on the college campus where she taught museum management. But the man walking down the train aisle toward her knocked the breath right out of her chest. His strongly carved face, his height, and the sight of a sticky faced little girl resting her head on his broad shoulder made Azzie feel all warm and nesty. A cone of bright pink cotton candy danced precariously close to his fair hair and Azure had to stop her fingers from picking a piece of the feathery treat from behind his ear as he settled into the seat across from her. Mister Sexy brushed a glance her way, but quickly averted his green eyes.

A thrill of sexual awareness shivered down Azure's spine. *Get a grip!* She commanded herself. She knew there was no way a Plain Jane like herself would ever merit a first look from a man like him, let alone a second one. Azure settled into her seat and waited for the old steam engine to take her home. Half an hour later her contemplation of the Christmas lights in Outlaw Junction was interrupted by the sound of an erupting volcano spewing half-digested food all over the gorgeous hunk.

===#==#===

Hot liquid hit Rockford Hollister's lap a split second before a noxious smell flew up his nostrils. He knew giving Meghan a third cotton candy was a bad idea, but he needed her calm and happy on the long train ride around the lake.

His natural instinct to jump up was thwarted by little Meghan sprawled across his lap. He was stuck sitting in vomit and became immobilized by horror, while he fought his own gag reflex.

Rock had left the nanny behind in New York City and didn't know what to do. He had never been alone with his daughter before, and he certainly had never cared for her when she was sick. He had to wonder if she often got sick when traveling, and if she did, then her mother should have told him so before she had flown off on her own cruise.

He could hear other kids commenting around him and at least one person used the word gross. He had to agree. It was gross and he still didn't know what to do beyond trying to stifle his own reflexes.

They were on an old-fashioned steam locomotive in the middle of the Maine wilderness. Heading slowly to nowhere. Horror struck Rock as he realized there probably weren't any restrooms on this rattling rust bucket.

The rosy cheeked woman across the aisle jumped to her feet. Crap, did some of the puke hit her?

"Where's your diaper bag?" He looked up into a pair of dark brown eyes.

"Ize a big girl. No more diapers," Meghan lifted her tearstained face to proclaim.

"My goodness, you are a big girl." The woman smiled gently at his young daughter while she removed the fluffy pink scarf from around her neck and mopped the child's face with it. Rock almost jumped out of his seat when the woman's knuckles brushed against, no, he would not think about where her hand was. Since when did his body respond to an accidental touch from a stranger with an instant hard-on?

"Ize gonna be sick again."

"She is green. Does she often suffer from motion sickness?" Warm brown eyes glanced his way.

"I don't know." He watched as the warmth drained out of her look. "I don't usually travel with her. I'm keeping her while my ex is on a post-divorce cruise celebrating her freedom from her second husband."

"Marta says Mama has gone lookin' fer nother husband," Meghan proclaimed woefully.

"We're more than half an hour away from the station. The poor little thing is going to be sick the entire time if we don't get her off the train," the woman said quietly. "There's a stop up ahead, at an old Victorian village display. You can get off there and give her little tummy a chance to feel better."

"Is there a café there or a first aid station?"

"Good heavens, no," Brown Eyes dimpled. "This time of year there are a few small buildings lit up, but they are closed until after the spring thaw. People like to wander around the lake shore and sip lemonade on warm days."

"You want us to get out in the middle of nowhere in the snow? How will that help Meghan feel better?" He heard the hard edge in his voice, but Meghan was moaning again and he was afraid she was about to spew for the second time.

"Don't be silly," the woman chided. "We're almost at the guest cabins. I'm getting off at the depot there. Come to my cottage. We'll let the little sweetie rest for an hour. I'll give her some nice mint and ginger tea to settle her tummy and you can catch the last train back to the main depot. You'll be back on the road in less than two hours with a little girl that isn't throwing up anymore."

"I didn't realize they rented out the cabins in the winter." It wasn't hurting Meghan any if he got the four-one-one on some of the side tracks of the park, Rock justified to himself. After all, it was his reason for making this trek in the first place. Meghan would have been happy just to see the big tree outside Rockefeller Center.

"We do have a few cabins that are winterized. There are several writers and artists who like to immerse themselves in the peace of the woods when they're up against a deadline or want to start a new project."

"Or want to escape their wives?" He gave her a half smile.

"Or their husbands," she chuckled. He liked the rich, warm sound of it. "Yes, that could be one of the ingredients in the mix."

"Are you here to escape your husband?" he asked.

He watched a blush race up her face.

"No, I'm not." Her answer was bald and simple. He didn't know if she had a significant other or not, and he suddenly found himself wanting to know.

Before he could ask any probing questions, the train slowed down and squealed to a stop at a small depot. In the distance he could see Christmas lights outlining a dozen small sheds. Rock was dubious about taking Meghan into one of those small structures. While he debated the merits, the child opened her mouth and ejected the hot dog he had fed her for supper. His nose twitched at the smell as his leather jacket became covered.

He would not gag. Especially not in front of this Good Samaritan.

The woman with the pink scarf did not flinch nor did her rosy cheeks pale. She just patted Meggie's back and wiped the little girl's face with the scarf. He'd have to be sure to get her address so he could send her a new one when he got back to New York since his daughter was doing an excellent job of ruining this one.

The pragmatic part of him wondered if his jacket and jeans would ever be wearable again. However, he was surprised to discover there was a bigger part of him that didn't care. He just wanted his little girl to feel better.

Without another word, the woman lifted Meghan into her arms and headed for the door. The conductor opened the door and jumped down to place a set of wooden steps in the six inches of snow that covered the platform. The uniformed guy raised a set of white eyebrows at her.

"What are you doing with that child, young lady?" the elderly gent asked. From what Rock had observed most of the employees were either a few months away from collecting their Social Security checks or their high school diplomas. Though he seemed spry enough, this guy looked like he was already getting the monthly check.

"Poor little mite is suffering from a bad case of motion sickness and too many treats. I'm taking her to my place to settle her tummy," the woman answered with a smile warm enough to melt the old man's stern expression. "Pick them up at the whistle stop when the last train is coming through. With a steady seat and a little ginger tea, this little cutie should be fit to go by then."

"Young lady, your granddad isn't going to be too happy about you taking strangers to your place," the old man persisted. In Rock's opinion, the conductor showed more concern than what the situation and his position merited.

"By the time my grandfather finds out, these nice folks will already be home, tucked into their own beds." Brown Eyes showed a stiff backbone when faced with the old gent's interference.

"Satellite says it's going to snow all night. I'll expect you to be on that train as well."

"Thank you for your concern, Mr. Carmichael, but I'll be staying in my own home tonight."

As Rock passed the man he heard him mumble, "Stubborn woman."

Rock suppressed a shiver as Carmichael's stare drilled into him. The old man's warning was clear; he knew what Rock looked like. Any funny business and a good physical description would be going to the authorities. It was a good thing Rock only wanted the land and wasn't in the market for a woman. Certainly not one in the employ of the old curmudgeon who wouldn't talk to him, Rock didn't "do" business that way. The one solid piece of information he had picked up in the park was that all the employees were loyal to the Brown family.

Brown Eyes turned away from the train stop and the buildings trudged through the mounting snow towards the woods. She carried his daughter, a backpack slung over her shoulders, and a tote bag that looked heavy hanging from her arm. Rock reached for Meghan, but the child whimpered and clung to the woman's neck. "Let me take her, she's too heavy for you to carry through the snow."

"It's okay. We're doing fine. It's not too much further to my cottage." Meghan snuggled into her new friend's neck and glared at her father over the woman's shoulder.

Rock's heart twisted in his chest.

He hadn't spent much time with Meghan-- he had been too busy building up his business. Jenna, his ex-wife, had complained about Rock's hours. She wanted his money to spend, but she also wanted his attention. When the boredom of being a business wife set in, Jenna walked out. She didn't know she was pregnant until a month later. She refused to give their marriage another try. She didn't think her new boyfriend would appreciate it. As a result, Rock had never spent any time alone with the child. There was always a nanny around to make sure he never had to face anything as degrading as vomit in his lap. Even so, he didn't expect his daughter to prefer a stranger's arms to his. Unless he wanted to rip the child forcibly away from the woman, he would have to let the situation remain as it was and hope she wasn't some kind of crazy back woods axe murderer.

It was possible.

The woman might be a Stephen King devotee; how the hell did he know? In spite of the fear that Annie Wilkes might be carrying his child into the woods, he couldn't face his daughter's rejection again. Instead, he let Meggie stay where she was.

"At least let me carry your bags." He had to work to keep the snap out of his voice.

"That would be wonderful. Thank you," she said as she stopped to hand him the tote bag and shifted Meghan to her other shoulder while he took the back pack. "Here. You might need this."

She handed Rock a flashlight. When she once again turned her back and headed into the woods away from the lighted sheds, he used it to check the contents of the bag. He breathed a sigh of relief to see there were no axe handles protruding from them. Even curvy young women with rosy cheeks and warm brown eyes could be stark raving crazy.

He lived in New York where crazy people were plentiful.

Jenna, his ex-wife, was a good example. She looked like an angel, but was as crazy as a loon. Unfortunately, she was smart enough to hide her crazy side from most people, so he wasn't in a good place to go for primary custody. Until recently, he hadn't thought much about having Meghan fulltime. She had good nannies. She was always clean and well fed. But when he looked into her eyes she looked lonely. He didn't want his little girl to feel lonely.

For now, his number one priority was to make sure Meghan was all right, and someplace warm and dry. He hoped this wasn't a bigger mistake than coming to view the decrepit Brownville Junction Amusement Park and Train Museum at night, in a snow storm, alone, with a sick child.

He knew through his research that the park opened at dusk every night after Thanksgiving trying to cash in on the holiday spirit with a gaudy display of Christmas lights. He had underestimated how long it took to drive the slick roads of Maine, so they had arrived later then he had planned. Then there were the long lines waiting to get into the park and even longer lines waiting at the depot for the train. By the time it was his turn at the ticket window, all the early trains were booked and the only seats he could get were on the late train. It was well past Meghan's bedtime before they climbed aboard for the ill-conceived ride.

"If this is the last train, how can another one pick us up later?" He suddenly realized the flaw in her plan to nurse Meghan and let the train leave without them. *Great timing! Realizing when it was too late to jump back on the train. The whole crazy woods-woman scenario was beginning to take root. What kind of father allowed a complete stranger to walk off with his child?*

"We have staff at some of the exhibitions along the route. There is a special, no frills run to pick them up," she answered breathlessly. The exertion of walking through the snow, carrying the child, and talking must be getting to her. Or was the excitement of her nefarious plans for him making her breathless?

"I can take Meghan now," he suggested.

After they got out of this snow covered nightmare he was going to fire Nanny Marta and hire a new nanny who didn't get sick at inconvenient times. Then he was going to fly off to somewhere with a mean temperature of eighty plus. His leather jacket was fine for running in and out of cabs, but not so great trekking through the great outdoors in a snowstorm.

Ashley Briggs, the Briggs in Hollister & Briggs, had assured him the land was a piece of paradise, plunked into the middle of the wilderness. There would be no problem turning it into a four season resort. The snow sticking to his eyelashes and the rising wind had him thinking otherwise. Who would want to live in this environment, or even visit it?

Ashley had heard about the park and had sent someone in over the summer to check it out. Her investigators reported the park was a rundown pile that no longer attracted crowds. Hollister & Briggs would be able to pick up the land for a song. Then they would build a resort complex and exclusive vacation homes on it. She planned on turning it into the new Mecca of the rich and wealthy.

Rock wanted to check it out for himself before he put any more into a project he wasn't sure he wanted.

Now he wondered about Ashley's sanity when she assured him the land would quadruple their fortunes. He didn't see it. He was a city dweller through and through. Sure he enjoyed his beach houses, but no one could ever say the Hamptons or Palm Beach were away from the beaten path.

His foot slipped into a ditch and he realized in this place he couldn't even find the path, let alone the beaten path.

Horace Brown, the owner, refused to make the land accessible for viewing so they sent in a team to surreptitiously survey the land. Some old guy camping had seen the team and reported them. They had been arrested for trespassing. The team was jailed for a week before they were seen by a judge, then heavily fined.

It was obvious the old man had powerful friends in the area who were willing to look out for his interests.

Brown didn't respond to their overtures and was adamant about not selling. Even though the park was in dire financial straits, the old man refused to entertain an offer from Hollister & Briggs. Ashley had sent letters to his son and daughter so his heirs would know there was a lucrative offer. She had hoped they would persuade the old man, but so far, Hollister & Briggs hadn't received a reply from his children or from the old man.

Rock's team hadn't been able to provide him with pictures of the area. He had to rely on aerial shots and postcards from the gift shop, but the little he had seen of the land today had increased his hunger for the property. He wouldn't want to live here, but the lake and mountains were impressive. One of his investigators had heard the rumor there was a pretty waterfall on the property, but no local could or would tell him where it was located.

Horace Brown's opposition fed Rock's appetite to develop the land. It was an itch under his skin. The old coot was foolish to refuse to negotiate. Rock had seen the numbers; he knew the theme park was in financial trouble. All he had to do was wait another year or two for it to go bankrupt, but waiting was not in his nature. He wanted the land now.

Ashley was pushing hard for an early takeover. She'd had had some personal financial reverses and needed to recoup her losses as quickly as possible. She was so sure they would have the land, she had already begun soliciting bids from builders.

Once again his foot slid into a ditch and he pitched forward, narrowly missing a tree that was aimed at his head.

Brown Eyes still carried his daughter, and she was getting further ahead. The only illumination came from the nearby cottages that were rimmed in Christmas Lights and the flashlight he carried that glared on the snowflakes. He doubted the Park would make enough to cover the electric bill. He'd have a better understanding about what was going on after he got the woman to let down her guard and talk.

"Daddy, hurry and catch up," Meghan's trembling little voice carried to him from the trees. "We're gonna lose you in da dark."

It was terrible to see his little Meghan sick, but some good would come out of it. He was getting to see one of the cabins while he picked this woman's brain. It was obvious she knew a lot about the place. Inside information was always the best kind to have, and so far no other employee had talked.

He had to hand it to Horace Brown. The man knew how to gain the loyalty of his employees.

He hurried through the snow to catch up with his daughter. When he reached them he flashed a friendly grin at the stranger. "We should introduce ourselves, since you are making off with my daughter. My name is Rock and you are carrying Meghan." He decided at the last minute not to use his last name. In an enterprise of this size, rumors of his offer were flying rampant through the employees. This little gold mine of information might dry up if she connected him with Hollister & Briggs. He knew from listening to the people working the concessions, the employees didn't want the park to fall into the greedy hands of "flatlanders". He was afraid this woman might feel the same way.

They entered a clearing and a small gingerbread house covered in Christmas lights sat welcoming them. It was so tiny it looked like an old fashioned dollhouse and looked much smaller than the other places they had passed. Brown Eyes stepped onto the miniature porch, and turned to him with a smile as bright as the lights on the Christmas tree next to her. "I'm Azure. My friends call me Azzie."

Her radiant smile made his blood rush south once again and the cold air did nothing to inhibit his throbbing erection.

Azure. Azure Brown. Horace Brown's only granddaughter. He liked Azure. She sounded like a fun girl. Things couldn't have turned out better if Rock had planned it. According to his investigators she had left a teaching job in Boston to come help out with the park after Horace had some kind of medical problem.

Rock was willing to bet his Palm Beach house that Azure would be happy to see this place sold while there was still money to trickle down into her bank account. What young woman wanted to give up a career in a bustling city like Boston to live in the back of beyond? With her share of the money she could live in style.

The taste of victory was as sweet as Meghan's cotton candy on his tongue. He was a born salesman; if he couldn't sell this woman on the pleasures of returning to city life in the next hour, then he didn't deserve the Florida house.

Azure Brown threw open the door with a flourish.

Rock looked inside the "house". She had to be joking. She had lured him and his daughter to a shed in the woods. The place was too small to be a house. It resembled the false fronts people used for extravagant Christmas decorations. The interior had to be smaller than the guest lavatory in his Manhattan penthouse.

He was in the backwoods of Maine and no one other than an elderly conductor on an ancient train knew they were with this woman. Perhaps he was stuck in a Stephen King novel after all.

The woman preceded him into the building, turned up the interior lights which had been on dim, and said, "It should be nice and warm in here. The heat was set to automatically turn on half an hour ago and because the house is so tiny it doesn't take long for it to heat up."

If this was the best old man Brown could provide for his only granddaughter, persuading her to accept his offer wouldn't be any challenge at all. He'd add an offer of a real house near the lake as a vacation home. That should be enough enticement for her to get the old man to sign on the dotted line. With any luck, he would be back in New York on Sunday with the ink still wet on the contract.

Rock's mouth dropped open when he stepped into a pink and white cloud. His nose twitched as he smelled chicken soup. The place no longer looked like a shed, it felt like a home.

Perhaps the woman was a witch like in the old fairy tale, only instead of a house made of candy, she lured men in with soups and stews.

===#==#===

Ashley Briggs threw down the television remote in disgust. The weatherman predicted the possibility of snow, and all her friends had flown out of the city. She never stayed home on a Friday night, but no one was available to go out on the club circuit with her. There were no parties-- nothing.

None of her friends had called to see if she wanted to flee the city with them.

Rockford never bothered to show up in the office at all today. She had tried calling him several times, but he had shut his cell off and nobody answered his home phone, not even his housekeeper. The miserable bastard had probably flown off to Palm Beach with his latest bimbo.

That was unacceptable. They were business partners. If Rockford had planned on missing a day in the office, he should have consulted with her. What if she had set up a meeting with an important client?

Eventually she had her secretary, Merle, hang around the break room to find out what Rockford's secretary was telling the others. Merle came back with a preposterous story. Rumor had it Rockford was taking care of his daughter Meghan. It couldn't be true.

Ashley had spent months cultivating a "friendship" with Jenna. She had to be so careful with every word she said to the nitwit. It had taken time, but she had finally convinced the airhead that as the mother of a precious little girl, she had to have primary custody of the kid. Rockford could never be trusted alone with a child. After all, hadn't he neglected Jenna, his wife, throughout their entire marriage in favor of work?

Jenna hadn't been as easy to convince as Ashley had hoped. She had whined on forever about what a wonderful guy Rockford was. He would never do anything to hurt his child. Blah. Blah. Blah. She really hated Jenna.

Rockford's attachment to the kid still mystified Ashley, but at least she could use that little monster as a reason why they shouldn't produce any children after they married.

Chapter 2

"Leave your boots on the drying rack and take off your jacket," Azzie said as she stood Meghan on the floor just inside the door. She removed her own coat and hat and hung them on the hooks placed on the wall for that purpose. Then she picked the child up once again. While the man shrugged out of his jacket, she gently placed the little girl on the built-in chaise in her reading nook at the back of the house, took the child's jacket and boots off, and wrapped a warm pink afghan around her. "Rock, if you're cold you can stand near the heater. You'll warm up in a jiffy."

The kitchen table was a Murphy style in a wall cabinet near the nook. Azzie had closed it up when she left for the office that morning. She hated walking into a dirty table when she got home at night, and having the table out of sight gave the illusion of more space.

She pulled the table down with one hand and opened one of her two folding kitchen chairs with the other hand. Then she grabbed a round tin of saddle soap and some rags from a shelf set into the wall where the table had been. She handed them to Mr. Tall and Handsome.

He was a gorgeous creature— in a city dwelling, Colin Firth sort of way. His eyes were a sparkling green, with a come-hither message embedded deep within them. They were what her grandmother called bedroom eyes. "The bathroom is through that door. It's small but functional." She pointed to a door next to the nook. "My cousin left some sweats here on his last visit. They're on the top shelf. You can change in there. When you're through getting changed you can throw your jeans into this plastic bag. There are facecloths and towels on the shelves. I have to warn you that the water will be cold. I'll heat the kettle and add the hot water into the tank that services the vanity in a few minutes." Rock looked a little shell shocked. He eyed the tin in her hand dubiously. "You can use this saddle soap to clean your jacket when you come back out."

It took effort, but Azzie finally dragged her eyes off his and busied herself pouring water into her electric kettle. After she turned the kettle on, she ladled chicken soup from the crock pot on the counter into a soup bowl and set it aside to cool. She had known snow had been in the forecast and had thrown the ingredients into the pot before she left to catch the morning train. Nothing more comforting than a hot bowl of Granny's homemade chicken soup on a cold winter's night. It didn't chase away a bout of loneliness, but it did give comfort.

"Meghan, do your friends call you Meggie?" The little girl shook her head no. "Do you mind if I do?" The child smiled her answer. "Okay, Meggie, would you rather have ginger ale or a nice warm ginger tea?"

"Do you think it's wise to give her anything else to throw up?" Mr. Studly asked. He was obviously inept at dealing with the sick child.

"Ginger will help to settle her tummy," Azzie replied quietly. "Plus it's always better to have something in your stomach when you're sick. There's nothing worse than the dry heaves."

Azzie gave him a small smile before turning back to the stove. She could feel him watching her for a few moments before the bathroom door closed behind him. Upon hearing the door close she felt her muscles relax. In the presence of Mr. Handsome she had automatically sucked in her tummy to hide the few extra pounds she had gained since leaving the Boston gym behind last August. It was one of the few things she missed about city life.

It wasn't much of a sacrifice. Riding a bike for most of her transportation needs gave her legs and lungs good exercise, but didn't do much for her abs and no matter what she did, she still had her sizable butt.

"Sweetie, I'll be right back," Azzie said with a smile for Meggie. "I'm going up there to put on some dry clothes." She pointed to the staircase and loft above Meggie.

She returned a few seconds later with a stuffed rag doll her grandmother had made for her when she was younger than Meggie. Azzie wore her fuzzy sleep pants and her favorite oversized shirt. She knew she'd have to change again after she walked them back to the train stop, but that was okay—there was no way she could stay in her wet jeans any longer.

Her thoughts were interrupted when Rock returned to the room. He sat at the table, opened the tin of saddle soap, and awkwardly began cleaning the vomit from the leather. "Where are you hiding the horse?"

"Excuse me?" Was that a squeak Azzie heard in her voice? The sweats were the right size, but the way the sweatshirt clung to his broad shoulders made it difficult to get a sound out of her throat.

He held up the tin. "The horse that goes with the saddle."

Azzie felt the burn of her blush. She wasn't usually this obtuse. "There is no horse or saddle. At least not here. I use that to clean my own leather jacket and boots."

Her blush deepened when she realized she answered his teasing with a serious reply. *Awkward!* She wanted to bang her head against the wall. Once again her stilted social skills killed the conversation.

Rock worked on his jacket while Azure spoon-fed Meggie. Her quiet conversation with the child was interrupted by the chirp of a phone.

Azure grabbed the phone from her backpack before the second ring. "Azzie, the train just pulled in and Carmichael said he dropped you and some fella off at your place. He said you wanted the job train to pick the guy up," Adam Jenkins, the station manager, bellowed into her ear.

"That's right," Azzie replied.

"Sorry, girl, but there ain't gonna be another train tonight, snow is coming down hard. The tracks are covered, or will be soon, and visibility is zero. I can't send out the snow train in these conditions. The storm system picked up power over the ocean and now the weather channel is predicting blizzard conditions. The number eleven barely managed to complete her run. They were in a white-out. Carmichael said the engineer could barely find the tracks to get back home. They had to go so slow, it put them way off schedule."

"What are we going to do about our people still out in the field?" Azzie asked dully.

"They're already on their way in," Mr. Jenkins said. "Since the snow started before they reported to work, I sent them all out on snow mobiles."

"Oh dear. Will they be safe on them?" Guilt washed through her as she thought about the dozen people scattered around the train route riding snowmobiles back to the station in near white-out conditions. She had barely been able to see her way down her path for half the walk home. What if one of her workers got hurt? How would she live with herself?

"Don't worry, Azzie girl, they're all experienced riders. In fact, from listening to them talk they were more 'an happy to get a chance fer the first ride of the season. I was kinda wishing I was riding one myself, then I remembered my hip replacement surgery coming up next month and thought better of it. I can wait until after the sawbones is done with me." She could see Jacob Jenkins throwing down his cane and ripping the hat off his head to feel the icy wind whipping through his ancient afro. The mental picture brought a smile to her lips and made her momentarily forget her dilemma.

"The lake isn't solid yet. You did warn them not to travel on it?"

"Girl, I've known that lake since before you were born. Went skinny dipping there as a child. Of course I told them." She could hear the chuckle in Mr. Jenkins voice.

"I know, I'm a worrier," she laughed.

"Should we send a rescue team out there to pick up you and that strange fella you took home with you?"

Azzie's mind buzzed. She didn't want to have a strange man stay in her tiny house overnight, not even one as handsome as Rock. All the Criminal Minds episodes she had seen at least half a dozen times each flashed through her mind. Didn't most serial killers hide behind a pretty face and a genial personality?

Then Meggie called to her daddy and Azure knew she couldn't send a sick child out in the middle of a blizzard, especially when the only means of transportation would be an open snowmobile. What if Meghan was really sick and not just reacting to too much junk food and the bumpy train ride? "No thank you, Mr. Jenkins.

We'll be okay here. Batten down the park and anybody who's worried about the roads can stay at the inn or the motel tonight. My treat. Make sure anyone who does stay calls home before the phone lines go down on the entire town."

"Sure thing, boss." There was a brief pause. "You should also know that the wires are already down. Land phones and electricity are out. If you hadn't insisted on getting us these satellite phones I wouldn't have been able to call you at all and with the weather conditions worsening I'm not sure how good they'll work later. We're on generators until we get the park closed."

"Do you need me to come in?"

"Naw, you stay warm and safe," Adam Jenkins replied. "You have enough fuel for your generator? Don't want you running out of heat in that glorified shed you call home."

"We're still running on solar power, but if or when that's depleted, I have plenty of fuel to recharge the batteries," Azzie said. Her hand massaged the kink she always got in her neck whenever someone picked on her tiny home.

"Looks like we're in for a long nor'easter." Azzie heard the worry in her station manager's voice. "The weather guy said another storm joined the first one and it is now massive, slow moving, and ready to dump all she has on us."

"Don't worry, Mr. J. If I run out of fuel, the truck's fuel tank is filled and I can always recharge my batteries off of it. Worse comes to worse, I can use the old sled we keep in the maintenance shed," she said, referring to the old ski doo they kept in a line shack next to the whistle stop depot.

"Well, if you're sure you'll be okay, we're almost through closing down here. Except for a couple of the teens we have working, the rest of us are old hands at this. We'll just lock up and move everyone over to the motel."

"Okay. Thank you, Mr. Jenkins. Make sure you take all of the prepared food over to the motel with you. You know how people like to chow down when they're afraid there's not going to be enough to eat."

"Listen, young lady, there's no one staying in Cabin Three. We have it set up with supplies in case a work crew needs to bunker down. You can send that man over there. Don't let him stay in your place," concern made Mr. Jenkins' voice rough. Azzie had a warm spot in her heart for the elderly gentleman who had bounced her infant self on his knee as he steered Old Number Forty-Two down the tracks.

She released a pent up sigh. Brownville Junction didn't need the added expense of housing and feeding park employees and any stragglers that remained in the park. A blizzard would mean there would be no customers for at least several days and no way to offset the lost revenue.

If they lost the rest of this weekend, it only left her two weeks more to build up the accounts to the point where the creditors' bills could be paid. Could they get enough customers in those two weeks to keep the park from going into a bright red situation? Another red year would kill the park and Pop, too.

And that nasty bitch, her stepsister Ashley Briggs, would swoop in to steal the park from them.

She forced a smile on her face before she turned to face Rock. "Looks like you and Meggie are going to be my guests for the night. The snow has increased and it's thick on the tracks. We do have a snow train, but it won't be coming out tonight. We won't be able to get another train through until the snow stops." She hoped her voice sounded cheery—she didn't want to make a park customer feel as if he was an imposition, even though he was.

But what a sexy imposition, a tiny voice in the back of her mind taunted.

===#==#===

Ashley ignored her doorman as she stepped out of her building. Rock hadn't returned any of her calls and she had to find him.

He was in between "girlfriends", so unless he had gone out tonight to find a new one, he should be alone. There was absolutely no reason for him not to answer her calls.

If he had found himself another little slut she would kill him. It was her turn. She had waited patiently for him to realize that she, Ashley Briggs, was the perfect woman for him. She already had reservations for a romantic Christmas vacation. He was still fighting the attraction between them so she may have to hide her true intent under the guise of business, but once she got him to Tahiti and they were alone in the remote beach bungalow she had reserved, he would be hers.

But for now, the first order of business was to find him. She'd start by going by some of his favorite hunting grounds. He had to be on the hunt for his next little fling.

Ashley was not deterred by the snow that hit her in the face when she stepped out from under the awning. She just stepped back under the canvas canopy and turned her head to signal the door attendant to find her a taxi. After all, this was New York. A little snow wouldn't stop her from reaching her objective.

Chapter 3

Azure wasn't comfortable having a strange man stranded in her house overnight, no matter how hot he was, little Meggie made a good buffer, she hoped, but it was too late to worry about it now. She had played with the idea of taking them to Cabin Three, as per Mr. Jenkins instructions, but the walk would be difficult and their clothes were wet from the snow that had accumulated on them on the walk to her cottage.

The wind had become stronger and was howling through the woods. A gust of wind pounded the snow against the side windows. There was no way she could send that child back outside tonight.

Yes, they kept cans of meat, soup, and beans in the cabin, but the month of December had been extremely cold and they were probably frozen, the bottled water would be solid by now. There wouldn't be any fresh fruit for the little one to eat when she was feeling better, no milk for her cereal, no fluffy blankets to keep the poor little thing warm. Just a couple of sleeping bags and wool blankets which probably needed a good airing before a child could get near them.

If she took Rock and Meghan to Cabin Three they would have to carry food and blankets through the snow.

Not to mention the cabin was not as snug as her little house. There were drafts and probably small tenants had taken up residence in there since the last cleaning. Plus there was no electricity in that cabin. To put it nicely, the cabin was "rustic". It was scheduled for an overhaul next summer, when they would add solar panels and wiring, but that didn't make it habitable now for the father and child.

She also doubted Rock's ability to keep a fire going, and the fireplace and woodstove were the only means of heat and cooking Cabin Three had. Then she factored in her doubts about his ability to cook a healthy meal for his daughter. She already knew the man's child rearing skills needed a lot of work. *Better to let them stay in her place and minimize the possible liability,* she rationalized.

===#==#===

Meghan's pale face struck a note of guilt into the conscience Rock didn't know he had. He shouldn't have used her as an excuse to get into the park.

He couldn't deny he was pleased to find himself isolated with the one person who should know the property inside and out. The person closest to Horace Brown, his beloved granddaughter. However, his daughter's big eyes staring at him from her pale face touched a place deep inside him he didn't know he had. He had never felt so bad before.

He had to snap out of it and stop feeling guilty about the child. He had to concentrate on work. Otherwise this was a wasted trip, and Rock didn't waste time, not in his personal life and not in his work life.

Azure Brown had to know the park was nearly bankrupt. If he played this right she would be the one to convince her grandfather to sell the place to Hollister & Briggs. If the old man wouldn't listen to her, her own greed for a better life would convince her to take the steps needed to have the old man declared incompetent. The ebullient thrill of victory close at hand drowned out any paternal worry Meghan had raised in him. The sooner he got the conversation rolling, the sooner he would have the property in his portfolio. He had to find a way to start the conversation, but how? The woman was constantly hovering over his little girl.

"Does this happen often?" *Brilliant question, Rock, old buddy.* It was pretty bad when he wanted to slap himself up the side of the head. He really should have thought of a better conversation starter instead of blurting the first thing that popped out of his mouth.

"The snow or people getting stranded at my house?" Azure looked at him with a smile curling her lips, and there was a definite twinkle in her eyes that made his body aware of her as a woman. "This is Maine. It snows a lot here. In these mountains we practically have our own weather system. I've never had people stranded in my home before. I don't usually hijack customers and I have certainly never brought any into my sanctuary before."

But how many men have you entertained in this little nest? He wondered as his eyes dropped to her lush breasts. He tore his eyes away.

"This is your home? I thought it was just a functioning shack you kept stocked with supplies for the random worker?" When he saw the look on her face he could have kicked himself for saying the first stupid thing that entered his head. He had to keep his mind and his eyes off her body and pay attention to the business that led him here in the first place.

"A shack!" Azure gasped, her voice bristling. He knew he had made a big mistake when he heard the outrage in her voice. "I'll have you know that this is a well-constructed small house. It's been my home for twelve years. A shack! You make it sound like you expect it to collapse at any moment under the weight of the snow. I built this house myself and it is solid." She tapped on the wall. "It has weathered every major storm that has been thrown at it. In fact, it has handled the weather better than the cookie cutter houses those flimflam men who claim to be developers have erected all over New England. Those scoundrels charge hundreds of thousands dollars for houses built with inferior materials. Every year we're approached by at least one of them wanting us to sell them a chunk of land."

Her attitude did not encourage him, but he still continued with the conversation. He needed more information about this land.

"Are you sure some of them weren't honest businessmen wanting to provide good housing for people?" Rock felt a prickle at the base of his neck.

"A few years ago a grifter . . ."

"A grifter?"

"Sorry, it's an old carnie term for a swindler. When I'm home here at the Junction I tend to forget that most people are not up on the lingo."

Uh-oh. "What happened?"

"This awful man 'sold' large parcels of our land and we only found out about it when people showed up with forged deeds and construction vehicles. We lost a few trees before we managed to get them off our land, then we had to go to court to defend our right to hold onto our property." Her face was a delightful shade of pink, the spit and vinegar in her voice was doing marvelous things to his body. Women never spoke to him, or even in front of him, like that, at least not until he told them their time together was over.

Stop admiring the woman and keep her on topic.

"How did you manage that?"

"We called in the sheriff and she and her deputies removed the people from the property. But then those suckers took us to court trying to claim our land." Now her face was closer to red and it was the first harsh word he had heard come out of her rosebud lips, other than flimflam man.

"You won in court?"

"There were organized protests. People were trying to say we had no right to own so much land. The phony owners tried to blame the scam on us. They had even trumped up evidence for the newspapers. Then a bleeding heart judge felt bad for the people who were swindled. She felt that since we had so much land we should take pity on their plight and give them the land in exchange for one dollar," Azure Brown's tone left no doubt in his mind about her feelings on the subject.

"So a precedent has been set and the land has been broken up?" Why hadn't his team told him any of this? He was sure he could buy out a bunch of losers who had been swindled. Especially if the Brown's and their local supporters weren't welcoming, and he was willing to bet his penthouse overlooking Central Park that the locals weren't too happy to have the interlopers living there. He could imagine of old man Brown as a feudal lord ruling over the masses. It painted a vivid picture in his head.

"No." He could see the disdain on her face as it dripped in her voice. "We won on appeal."

They won? Wrong precedent had been set, but he had the best lawyers in the world. He was sure his New York firm would be able to wipe a bunch of country bumpkin lawyers out in a courtroom situation.

"How did you manage to keep everything so quiet? I would think a scam like that would hit the headlines." He continued to polish his clean jacket while she bustled in the refrigerator.

"It helps to have expert researchers involved," she smiled innocently at him. "Someone unearthed the fact that the judge had a half-sister who had a daughter whose husband had been taken by one of the fake deeds. When that little fact was made known to the Justice Department, the judge was given the opportunity to resign rather than go through a misconduct trial. As part of the deal to keep criminal charges from being filed, all the trespassers agreed to quietly go away— it was that or go to jail as co-conspirators. I don't know if it was right, or even legal, the way it was handled. It didn't feel like it to me, but the Justice Department didn't want to face another scandal at that time. So they chose to sweep it under the rug. We were just happy to have our clean title back."

Azure set a large pot of something on the stove. "I want to save the chicken soup for Meggie in case she is really sick with a bug. I hope you like corn chowder. I have a lot left from last night. It's warm and it's filling."

At the mention of his daughter's new nickname, Rock glanced to see what she was doing and saw she was playing with a rag doll. He wondered where it had come from.

"If you don't like corn chowder, I'm sure I can find something else you will like." Azure looked at him expectantly.

"Never had it, but I do like Manhattan clam chowder," he said as he carefully put the cover back on the saddle soap.

"Yuck!" She crinkled up her cute little pixie nose. "I hate seafood."

"I thought everyone in Maine lived on seafood."

"They do, especially those that live by the coast, but I don't. My mother took me to eat in this swanky restaurant and ordered chowder and lobster for me. I ended up with a bad case of food poisoning. Never again have I touched seafood." She raised her hand as if taking an oath.

That meant he wouldn't be taking her to his favorite restaurant to celebrate after they closed the deal. He'd have to take her to Angelo's on Mulberry. She'd like the restaurant, it was trendy, the food was impeccable, and it was intimate. They could have some *Capezanna* and stuffed cannelloni, and then desert would be waiting for them back at his place.

Since when did he think about taking a woman back to the penthouse? Rock liked taking his women to expensive hotels with good room service. He could leave anytime he wanted and he wasn't stuck trying to push a clinging woman out the door on his way to work.

This woman fascinated him. Her gentle voice. Her warm brown eyes. Her lush curves.

It hadn't escaped his notice that Azzie had changed clothes while he was in the closet she called a bathroom. On the train she had worn jeans that had highlighted the wonderful curve of her ass, but since they had entered the little house she had changed into fleece pants. He wanted to run his hand over the pants and see if they were as soft as they looked. If she was as soft as she looked.

He quickly placed his jacket on his lap when she suddenly turned away from the stove to look at him.

"You must be finished by now. Let me hang that up for you." She reached for his jacket.

His raging hard-on pushed against the leather. The soft fleece lined sweats did nothing to hold the damn thing down. He should have worn briefs instead of boxers. At least there would have been some containment.

"No. No, that's okay. I still haven't warmed up from the snow yet." He sounded like a wimp, but it was better than letting her see the flag pole in his lap.

"You must have taken a chill. I'll turn up the heat. This house is little so it warms up quickly. I insulated it with sheep wool, and if you find a draft I'll give you a ten year family pass to the park."

"You're sure the park will be here in ten years?" He kept his voice casual. He was grateful she had given him an opening so early in the conversation. Maybe if he got his mind back into business mode and he stopped looking at her nicely rounded breasts under her scoop-necked tee-shirt his cock would stop throbbing. She had magnificent cleavage.

"Of course we'll be here in another decade. We're not going anywhere. Sure, the big name theme parks have hurt us over the years with their death defying roller coasters and their blockbuster movie themes, but we have our charms." She glared at him.

Women never glared at Rock. Simpered? Yes. But they never glared. He liked that spark in her chocolate eyes.

Rock ruthlessly shut down the confusing sexual urges and cast the smile women always called wicked her way. He shifted in his seat and whispered, "Yes, you certainly do have your charms."

Good. He'd made her blush. He was getting to her. If he kept her off balance she wouldn't see where this conversation was leading and in an unguarded moment she was liable to let slip some vital information.

She had tilted his world sideways by insulting his business and his first response was a desire to kiss her. Flimflam man! She sounded as old as her grandfather. As long as he kept her blushing and thinking like a woman he would have his way. He'd have the information he wanted and that would lead to him getting the land.

Chapter 4

That was the last sane thought he had that night.

While he cleaned his jacket, which he found amazingly soothing, he got a good look at his surroundings. His first impression of a pink and white cloud remained intact. Everything in the place was pink or white, except for the red roses on the counter and Azure's face.

She sat on the cushions next to Meghan and hand fed the child until Meggie shook her head and refused to eat any more. Then Azure bustled around closing heavy, pink drapes. Rock had the surreal feeling he had entered the pink and white world of his daughter's doll house.

Meghan was cocooned in an alcove that surrounded her on two sides with windows covered with white ruffled curtains and light rose-colored velvet drapes, the third side was a wall that separated the miniscule "bath" from the rest of the "house", while the fourth side was left open. Ruffles rippled from the edge of the seat (or was it a bed?) that Meggie reclined on. Shelves and fussy little pillows rimmed the cushion that completely filled the alcove. Even the Christmas tree on a small table near a rocking chair was pink!

He watched as Azure efficiently helped his daughter out of her vomit filled clothes and into a pink "Hello Kitty" tee-shirt. Now even his little girl was encased in pink.

The entire place screamed out "girly-girl"!

Rock rolled his shoulder muscles, trying to release the tension he felt. He didn't do girly-girls. He liked his women to have mature, sophisticated tastes and short tight skirts. Preferably in black.

Azure Brown plumped the pillows around Meghan before sitting on the edge of the cushions. He caught the occasional word of a murmured story about a train struggling to chug up a mountain. Meghan's eyes closed and her breathing evened out long before the story was finished.

"Give me your clothes."

"Huh?" That was the last thing Rock expected to hear from the woman who suddenly stood next to him.

"Give me your clothes. I'll wash them along with Meghan's. We don't need the aroma of vomit permeating the house all night." She held her hand towards him.

She had nice hands with long fingers that he wanted to see wrapped around his cock. *Where the hell did that thought come from?*

She must have been able to read his mind because her face flamed red with a blush that looked hotter than the flames in the gas heater behind her.

"Don't tell me you have a washing machine in this place, it's barely big enough to hold the three of us, and Meggie is only a tiny little thing." Rock knew he had insulted her again by the sparks that heated up her molten chocolate eyes. She had a short fuse when it came to this shed in the wilderness.

"I not only have a washer, I also have a dryer. Now give me your clothes."

He handed Azure the folded pile of clothing and watched her pivot on her heel. She turned to the kitchen area and pushed back the curtains, pink of course, under the counter.

Low and behold there were two pink appliances. "I didn't know they came in pink?"

"Amazing, isn't it? And they match the refrigerator and stove perfectly." Her smile beamed.

A few minutes later he raised his eyes from the leather jacket he was still cleaning to find her standing next to him with a flashlight in her hands.

"I'll be back in a few minutes. You have to decide where you're going to sleep tonight."

"I thought Meghan and I were spending the night here?" Was she about to toss them out into the snow? Although he suddenly felt like a frightened boy, there was no whine in his voice. He hoped.

She put the flashlight down on the table and sat on the futon an arm's length away. Tucked under the staircase, it was surrounded by shelves of books and ceramic trains. She pulled on her boots and laced them up. "You can either open this futon to sleep on or you can sleep in my guest loft." She pointed to a ladder he hadn't noticed before. It led to a loft that had sheer pink fabric and white Christmas lights twinkling from behind them.

Was that a chandelier hanging up there? The woman had actually hung crystal chandeliers in a shack!

"The choice is yours, but I would prefer it if you slept on the futon. It's not as comfortable as the guest bed, but you'll be closer to Meggie if she wakes up." She finished tying her boots and stood up. "It's scary enough to be sick away from home, but then to wake up in a strange place and not have her daddy nearby," her voice trailed off as she shook her head. She slipped into a ski jacket and pulled a wool hat over her ears. "I wouldn't want her to bump into the heater or wander out the door in the middle of the night."

There was something vulnerable in her eyes when she talked about Meggie needing her daddy nearby. He felt dishonest for not telling her that Meghan would rather have her paid nanny than him.

"Where are you going?" He wasn't panicking at the thought that this strange woman was leaving him alone with the child he barely knew, in the middle of the woods, in a blizzard. He was a man and men didn't panic over the simple stuff like taking care of a sick kid or a howling wind in the woods.

"It's snowing pretty hard and we've been using a lot of energy since we got home. I'm just going to check the battery levels and switch the leads if I have to. I also want to make sure there's enough propane left to keep the heat going all night."

He couldn't believe she could announce the fact that they might freeze to death so calmly.

"Let me get this straight. You brought me and my daughter into the middle of the woods so that we could freeze to death overnight?"

She snorted in response. She actually snorted. No woman he knew would ever issue such a sound in a man's presence. At least not in the presence of a man she hoped to impress.

"No one will freeze to death in this house overnight. It's well insulated and holds the heat inside fairly well, as long as we don't keep opening and closing the doors or windows. If the gas tank is low I will exchange the canister for a full one. The electricity is due to solar-powered batteries. I have several that are fully charged. I just have to move the leads."

Solar powered batteries in Maine, in winter, in the middle of a snow event. The woman was nuts. Solar energy was only reliable in the desert. Everybody knew that.

"Don't worry. If we go through all my solar reserves, I still have JIC." Apparently she was still reading his mind.

"JIC?"

"My 'just in case' generator. JIC. My Pop was a cynic about solar energy in New England too and insisted I had to have JIC." Then, without another word, she opened the door and disappeared into the cold darkness of the out-of-doors.

===#==#===

Half an hour later, a gust of cold wind hit Rock where he sat at the kitchen table. He knew it had been half an hour because he had checked his watch with the time on an antique clock once every thirty seconds since she left. The longer she was gone the more he worried about her. He had spent the last twenty-seven minutes convincing himself that he couldn't leave Meghan alone while he went out to find their hostess.

Relief swept through him as Azure stomped her way back into the house. Heavy wet snow covered the woman from head to toe. The only points of color were in her rosy cheeks, bright red nose, and a red checkered piece of cloth that covered a basket in her hands. The hands that had been empty except for the flashlight when she went out.

She shed her outer clothing near the door and hung them on hooks. She placed her boots on a mat, and then his heart stopped as she reached under her large top and pulled down the fuzzy pants. "It's coming down really heavy now, and there is zero visibility. If I didn't know where it was and I didn't have a great sense of direction, I would never have been able to find the truck. Nor could I see the house from the truck, even with all the lights blazing."

He felt like a perv, watching, in hopes of getting a peek at her rounded butt, but he was doomed to failure. When untucked from her waistband, the woman's shirt reached her knees.

Azure walked over to the gas heater and stretched her hands out to it. Rock tore his eyes off her shapely pink calves, barely noticing the pink heart socks. Her hands were red and fragile-looking from the cold. "It's a good thing you and Meggie are staying here. Mr. Jenkins wanted to send the rescue team out on snowmobiles, but it would have been dangerous for them and you to be out on the machines tonight."

"You're sure we'll be able to stay warm in here?" Rock asked, his concern for his daughter escalating by the minute. If Azure's hands were so cold in spite of the thick mittens she had worn, it must be brutal outside.

Azzie walked into the "bathroom" area and came back out holding a couple of towels. She went over and laid them on the floor under her dripping clothes, with a plastic trash bag under them. "Don't worry. We're fine here. We have plenty of power and more than enough food. We could survive the entire winter if we had to."

She was kidding, right? No one got stuck in the middle of nowhere for the entire winter, did they?

"The clothes are finished washing. I'm going to throw them into the dryer and turn the heater down. No sense wasting the gas on both when the dryer is going to steam this place right up." She ducked into the kitchen area.

This was a nightmare! Trapped in an overgrown shed with his little daughter and a sexy woman he couldn't touch.

When she walked back into touching range, his fingers itched to creep under the bottom of her shirt and see what she wore underneath. Azure looked at him and smiled. "Are you hungry? Would you like something to eat before we go to bed?"

His mind had conjured a vision of her naked and using the time honored way a woman had of keeping a man hot.

"Excuse me?" Did she just invite him to sleep with her?

"I'm going to have an apple tart and some tea before I go to bed, but if you prefer a sandwich or some more chowder, I can fix you some before I head up to my loft."

"An apple tart?" he asked, still dazed at the prospect of sleeping with this woman.

"Okay, an apple tart it is. What would you like to drink with it? I have milk, juice, soda, or tea."

What he needed was a shot of whiskey.

"Milk is good." When was the last time he drank a glass of milk? The chowder was good, but he had to admit, he could use more to eat. Maybe if he satisfied one hunger he would get his mind off his sexual hunger. He felt like a perv having those thoughts with his child sleeping in the same room.

"Do you want it cold, or would you like me to heat it up to help you sleep? I know the futon isn't the most comfortable place to sleep, but it's only for tonight. We don't want Meggie to wake up in a strange place and think she's alone," Azure said as she economically went about getting the items from the "kitchen."

Of course. He had forgotten all about the futon. He asked for cold milk and wondered where his lascivious thoughts were coming from, Azure was not a homely woman, but neither was she a spectacular beauty like the women he usually bedded. Her care and attention to Meghan had shown she had a warm heart and a gentle nature. No one else on that train made a move to help, or even offer any suggestions. Maybe this forced foray into fatherhood had him needing a mommy as much as his daughter did.

Azure placed the milk in front of him and pulled another folding chair down from the hook on the ceiling. She sat at the table with her tea and the plate of warm apple tarts.

He took a bite of his tart and rolled his eyes as the warm cinnamon sauce rolled over his tongue and dribbled out of the corner of his mouth.

"I'm sorry. I hope they haven't gone stale. I made them the day before yesterday." She fumbled with her fork. "They're good enough for me, but . . ."

"Lady, I haven't tasted anything this good in years." And he hadn't. Rock usually avoided sweets. He didn't have a lot of time for the gym so he tried to stay away from desserts to avoid getting a paunch like his father had developed working behind a desk all day.

A smile radiated from Azure's soul. Or at least that's what it looked like to him. Apparently she didn't get a lot of compliments. He should be able to get her on his side with a few well-chosen words. So why did he feel disappointed at the thought of flirting with her in order to get her property? Rock shouldn't have to remind himself he had a goal to work for. He was a businessman, first and foremost. Nothing was more important than the deal. Not even this young woman's feelings.

Before he could set his plan in motion, Azure drew him into a conversation about the past baseball season. He knew that Red Sox Nation covered quite a bit of territory, but he never realized it encompassed the north western mountains of Maine, closer to Quebec than to Boston, or one little teacher stuck in a tired old amusement park.

As soon as they were finished eating, Azure gathered the dishes and quickly washed them. Then she retrieved sheets and blankets from a drawer under the futon, adjusted the piece of furniture into a bed, and made it up for him to sleep on. Rock watched her as she bent over his bed, tucking in sheets. He wondered what she had on under that damn shirt. It never lifted enough to show him and he felt like a creeper watching to see if it would.

"You should be warm enough, but if not, there is an afghan on the back of the rocker." She pointed to the white rocking chair with a pink fuzzy blanket in the opposite corner. "I'm shutting off all the lights, except for a nightlight in the nook area for Meggie. I want to conserve power. We have more than enough, but I'm a Maine Yankee, I believe in making sure I am well prepared." Azzie's smile once again caused Rock's blood to migrate south. "I'm leaving you this battery operated lantern. If you're not ready to go to sleep yet, it's good to read by. I have plenty of books, so there should be something you'll like. If you prefer to use an e-reader, I have a spare one on the shelf to the left of the futon. It's fully charged. I'm going to head up to bed now. Is there anything else you need?"

"I can't think of anything." He had never seen anyone handle two unexpected guests so smoothly or to see to their comfort, at least not without several servants doing all the work. He'd like to have her in his employ. Perhaps as his PA, or a supervisor of special projects, or as his mistress. Once again he was surprised at how his thoughts kept turning to sex when he looked at Azure's well rounded figure.

===#==#===

Ashley fumed. Three-thirty in the morning and Rockford still hadn't returned her calls. She had been calling both his penthouse and his cell phone all night and he didn't answer the damn phone. She had even called his office line.

"Hey, lady, ya still gotta pay me. Cash or card, I ain't particular, but ya better include a good tip. I've been hauling your ass around for the last hour." Ashley's thoughts were rudely interrupted.

The nerve of the cabby! How dare he speak to her like that? Ashley was tempted to climb out of the cab and disappear into her building, but the guy looked brutal enough to follow her and she didn't trust the fool on the door to protect her.

Ashley used her card to pay him, but she did not add a tip. She did not reward insolent behavior. She also made note of his medallion number. She was going to report the man.

She wasn't ready to go back to her own place. She didn't like the idea of spending the rest of her night alone. What she really wanted to do was to go back to Rockford's building and bang on his door until he answered it. She'd rip off her clothes and he wouldn't be able to help himself. A thrill ran through her at the thought of him taking her up against the door. She would finally have her man.

Unfortunately, this cabbie was a cretin and there weren't any other cabs trolling the neighborhood. A few snowflakes and everybody had disappeared.

Ashley considered her options. Rockford's building was much too far for her to walk, the snow would ruin her beautiful Dolce and Gabbana lace and crystal heels. The city should have someone out clearing the streets and sidewalks, especially in her neighborhood. She should be receiving much better services for the amount she paid in taxes every year.

She opened the door of the yellow cab and stepped onto the sidewalk. Her heel slid on the slippery edge of the curb. The damn awning did not extend all the way to the street. She'd have to talk to the Owners Association about getting a better cover.

Chapter 5

Saturday morning dawned, but there was no sun. Nothing to be seen except white sky, white earth, and heavy white stuff weighing down the surrounding trees, when you could see the trees. The snow continued to fall from above. It swirled around the tiny house before it landed on the growing layers.

Azure was up bright and early with a big pot of oatmeal bubbling on the stove. Rock rolled off the futon. He had never spent a more uncomfortable night in his entire life. The futon was much too short for him. It didn't help at all that he was worried about Meggie and tried to stay alert in case she needed him, or tried to escape from the doll house.

Plus he had a strange feeling that made him toss and turn all night. If he didn't know himself better he might think he was feeling guilty about not telling Azure who he really was. But it couldn't be that. He was a businessman, a hot shot wheeler dealer from the business capital of the world, New York City. He didn't have anything to feel guilty about. He wanted this land. It wasn't anything personal. He wasn't out to hurt anyone. It was just business as usual.

Once again the table near the nook area that Meghan had slept in was used for the meal. They ate hot cereal with chopped apples and a good dollop of real maple syrup, which Azure said was made on the property and sold only in their gift shop. They didn't have to worry about any artificial ingredients.

"I have to go out and shovel a path to the truck and the chicken coop," Azzie announced as she placed the last dried dish on the shelf. "I'll put a movie on for you two to watch."

"You have cable out here?" Rock asked.

"We have cable at the hotel, the Inn, and my grandfather's house, but not for the cabins. Sorry," she said with a shrug of her shoulders. "However, I must admit that I have an obscene obsession with musicals and holiday flicks, so I have a wide selection for you to choose from." She handed him a cordless keyboard. "The television and the computer are connected. Just click on the menu and I'm sure you'll find something appropriate for Meggie."

With a click the screen came to life and the horrors of *Frosty* and *Santa Claus* flashed in front of his eyes.

"I'd be happy to shovel for you," he volunteered.

"That's sweet of you, but it is just as easy for me to do it myself as it is to tell you all the areas that must be done," she answered.

"No, no. I'm not being sweet," he denied the charge. "I'm used to leading a very active life and sitting in here while you are out shoveling all those cubits of snow isn't right."

Azure laughed. "Now I know you are being chivalrous."

He smiled through his gritted teeth as children's voices started singing about a top hat. "Please let me do this for you. You've been so busy taking care of us that you haven't had a chance to sit down and enjoy your day off."

"Okay. I'll allow you to be my knight errant." She turned to a shelf over the rack where the coats were hanging. When she turned back to face him she held a red knit hat, scarf, and mittens. "I have an old work jacket of Thawe's stored out in my truck. Unfortunately, our snow shoes are also out there. I didn't think to grab them last night and now I can't get to it until after the path is shoveled. You'll have to wear your nice jacket and leather boots. If you wait here, I'll run up to my loft and get you some wool socks. They will help to keep your feet warm."

He hadn't considered his handmade leather boots when he made his offer. Oh well, there were some sacrifices a man had to be prepared to make if he wanted to succeed in business. He just hadn't realized his Italian boots would be one of them. He had already written off the jacket as soon as Meggie spewed all over it last night.

Azzie returned a few moments later and held out a pair of heavy grey socks. "The hat, mittens, and socks are all wool. They will keep you toasty warm. Keep them on while you're outside. Even if you feel warm from the exertion. We don't want you to get a case of frostbite."

He sat on the kitchen chair and pulled on the socks.

"The first thing you have to do is shovel a clear path, at least a yard wide around the entire house. I want to make sure there is plenty of space for the exhaust from the heater to dissipate." Then she pulled aside the drapes on the window on the right side of the house. "Then if you shovel toward those two trees with bird feeders hanging on them, you will be on the right path to the truck and the chicken coop."

Rock now had his boots and jacket on. Azzie wrapped the scarf around his neck and he suddenly felt like the knight errant she had just teased him about. She smiled up at him and he wanted to slide his fingers over her makeup free face. Her naked, dewy lips tempted him to kiss her.

"Daddy, can I come out too?" Meghan's voice was the dash of cold water his boiling libido needed.

"Not right now, sweetie. We have to give your daddy a chance to make room for us out there first," Azzie laughed as she walked over to the restored futon. "Let's watch the movie. Would you like to cuddle with me for a while? I always liked snuggling with my grandmother while we watched Christmas movies."

Lady, I'd like to do more than cuddle with you, Rock thought as he walked out the door and into the blustering swirl of snow.

Rock hadn't shoveled snow since he was twelve years old and he had gotten in trouble for some minor infraction. His father had cut off his allowance and Rock was supposed to go on a ski trip with his school to Aspen. His father had already paid, but he refused to give Rock any spending money. Rock couldn't show up broke, so the only recourse he had was to go out shoveling with the housekeeper's son. He was surprised to find he actually enjoyed the manual labor.

It had taught him the value of earning your own money, and he always made sure his workers were well paid. They may not be as loyal as these Mainers were to old man Brown, but he knew they did a fair day's work for a fair day's pay.

He was no stranger to hard work, however rural Maine was a shock to the New York City resident. He was born and raised a New Yorker. The city boy in Rock was surprised to hear that people still raised their own chickens. It was an alien concept to him. If you wanted eggs you had them delivered. You didn't raise them yourself. Didn't homegrown eggs go out in the early twentieth century along with bustles and handlebar mustaches?

He was just about finished with the path to the chicken coop when a missile hit the back of his head. Rock stumbled and turned, opening up his face to another missile. He cleared the snow away from his eyes to find Azure with her arm pulled back, ready to pitch another snowball at him. His daughter was holding her belly and laughing merrily at him. He stared at Meghan and saw her rosy cheeks and bright eyes, and a happiness he had never observed in her before, right before another snowball hit him between the eyes.

He sent a light barrage of snowballs at Meggie and Azzie. After Rock allowed another snow ball to hit him he lunged at the two girls and carried them into the snow bank his shoveling had created.

They wrestled and squirmed under the weight of his body. His lips hovered near Azure's for an endless moment while he was tempted to kiss the smiling sweetness.

An icy rivulet ran down his spine. It took him a moment to realize that Meggie had squiggled her way out from under him and had dumped a big wad of snow down the neck of his jacket.

She giggled as she ran down the path he had dug. He followed her and caught up with her in front of the house. He scooped her high into the air. "You little demon. I think I should hang you on top of one of the trees and turn you into a Christmas angel."

"I don't think she can be an angel and a demon all in the same breath," Azzie laughed at him.

"Well, if anyone can do it, it's this little monkey," Rock growled through his smile.

"Daddy, what's a demon?" Meggie asked as she placed her mittened hands over his cheeks.

"That would be you, my sweet little daughter, when you are doing some not so nice things to your poor old dad," he chuckled at her.

"So Azzie is a demon too acuze her put a snake in her Mommy's bed?"

"Oh. Now I can see that Miss Azzie is a bad influence on you." He flashed a smile at Azzie. "What other nasty little tricks has she told you about?"

"She once tied her cousin's sneakers all together and her knots were soooo tight he had to cut da laces off and go ta school with his sneakers falling off his feets whenever he walked in dem," Meggie giggled. "Daddy, how come I doesn't have no cousins?"

"Your mother and I are both only children. In order to have cousins you need to have aunts and uncles," he replied. "I'm afraid you don't have any cousins."

"Oh. I want a baby sister."" Meggie giggled.

"Maybe someday, but not today," Rock answered. He had a sudden vision of Azzie with a baby on her shoulder. He knew fatherhood would be a different experience if he shared the parenting with her.

"Daddy, can we make Frosty?" Meggie's change of subject was a relief.

Rock sadly shook his head and said, "I don't know, honey. I'm not sure we have enough snow to do that."

"Silly, Daddy. We gots lots of snow."

They laughed and teased as they rolled the snow into the perfect sized balls to build a seven foot snowman.

"I think we may have to make this guy a little smaller," Rock said, "if we want to be able to put a hat on him and a face."

Meghan lost her smile.

"Rock, he doesn't have to be smaller, all you have to do is lift Meggie up on your shoulders and then she can put the hat on him and make his face." Rock had spent a good portion of last night and today wanting to kiss Azzie, but as he watched Meggie's face turn from despair to jubilation it was all he could do not to hug the woman.

He never hugged women. Had sex with them, yes. Hugged them affectionately, no.

"Hold on a minute while I run to the truck. I have a few things in there that Mr. Snowman needs." Azzie ran off before he could grab her. He wondered if the urge to hug her would return later, or if it was just a passing abnormality.

Rock and Meggie gathered tree branches to use for the snowman's arms. They were arguing over the placement of them when Azzie returned wearing a top hat and carrying a basket of mysterious stuff.

"I brought some coal for his eyes, cranberries for his mouth, and a carrot for his nose," Azzie held the basket under Meggie's wide eyes. The child wrapped her arms around Azure's legs. "Rock, why don't you lift Meggie up so she can make the face?"

Under Azzie's expert tutelage he carefully balanced Meghan on his shoulders while she shoved the ingredients for Frosty's face onto the top section of snow. It was a face that could have been created by Picasso, but Azure stood next to them applauding each and every misplaced article.

Finally, Azzie handed the top hat to Meggie who had to stretch up high to place it on the snowman's head. Rock lost his balance and stumbled. They almost crashed into their creation, but at the last minute Azzie grabbed him by the neck of his jacket and they fell into the snow pile in back of them instead. As he looked up, a piece of ice near the snowman's eye caught a light beam and winked at him.

"Ohhhhhhhhh," Meggie said.

"I think he needs a scarf." Azure removed the red and black striped scarf from around her neck and danced around the snowman while she wrapped the thing between the top and middle sections.

Meggie laughed and giggled nonstop. "Daddy, now the snowman needs a mommy and a little girl. He looks really sad standing there all by hizself." Did his daughter see him as a sad, lonely man standing by himself?

Surely not.

No one would ever mistake him for anything other than what he was—a happy, prosperous playboy.

When they returned to the tiny house that was becoming strangely comfortable to him, the girls made cookies while he pretended to read a mystery book he had found on one of the book shelves. He enjoyed eavesdropping on his daughter and the warm-hearted woman who had made them hot chocolate from scratch. He hadn't even realized it could be done that way. He stocked packets near the office coffee maker for his secretary who loved nothing better than chocolate and a romance novel. She kept them well hidden, but he knew they were there. Donna worked hard; she had earned a little leeway.

While the girls were cooking he searched through the books for something to do. Azzie's home was small, but she had more books crammed into her one-hundred something square feet than he had in all his properties combined. As a boy he had loved reading, but now he didn't have time to read for pleasure. He read financial reports in order to find more ways of increasing his wealth and that was it. He worked and he partied.

Introspection was depressing, so he dragged his thoughts back to the book. At first it was difficult to get into the story, but eventually the words on the page captured his attention and he was thrown into a world of intrigue while the aroma of cookies baking engulfed him. The sound of his child singing Christmas Carols filled the empty spots in his soul he hadn't known existed until his heart expanded with the wonder of it all.

The world felt right.

He felt like he had finally found home.

===#==#===

Where the hell was Rockford? Ashley hadn't seen or spoken to him since they left the office on Wednesday. Then that inept secretary he pampered informed her on Thursday that he was taking a few days off from the office to spend with his daughter.

His daughter! Yeah right. Jenna was a whore. Everyone knew that, but would Rockford listen to her and insist on having a DNA test? No! Not he. He would not even consider a woman might have sex with another man when he was there.

Ashley would bet half her fortune, if she still had one to bet, that little brat was not his.

She picked up a slice of cold pizza from the table in front of her. It was as appetizing as cold gravel, but she was only able to find one eatery willing to deliver to her, and all they had was pizza and pasta. She never let "food" like that cross her lips, but the guy on the phone informed her that his lights had been flickering and would probably go out soon, so if she needed food she had better order enough to last her for a while.

She grimaced at the horror of starches that perched on her tables. The man was obviously a savvy businessman. She was willing to bet he had emptied his refrigerators and overcharged her for the food and the delivery costs.

An hour after the food was delivered, the electricity in Ashley's building went out and she had to summon the maintenance man to light her gas fireplace for her.

Where the hell was Rockford? He still was not answering his phones. He should have been here to help her, or better yet, he should have had her over to his penthouse. His pantry was always well supplied and his housekeeper was a decent cook, or so he always told her. Not to mention his view of Central Park would be spectacular with everything coated in snow.

At least for a while.

Personally, Ashley did not care for snow, especially in her city. If she wanted snow she would go to Aspen or Saint Moritz, though her choice vacation spots included sun, sand, and surf.

Chapter 6

Azure allowed Meggie to help her make lasagna for dinner. While it baked in the small oven, the two girls played cards. Rock put down his book to help his daughter with her Fish hand. He was impressed with how quickly the child picked up the game. Before the game started he hadn't known she could recognize both the numbers and the letters for the court cards. He'd have to remember to play Fish with her when they were in the city and they returned to their visiting day routine. Maybe it was time to insist on having Meggie on the weekends, or at least every other weekend. She was quite a character and he was going to miss her when she was with her mother.

The lasagna was delicious, although he found his third helping was sitting heavily in his stomach. He had to pass up the poached pears Azzie produced for dessert as a result. He'd never had poached pears. It wasn't something the restaurants he frequented served.

After dinner the three of them shared the futon, which was once again set up as a couch, and watched Christmas movies until Meggie fell asleep. Rock carried Meggie to the "reading" alcove and Azzie covered her with a homemade blanket. She placed a folding screen in front of it to block the area off from the rest of the living space. It didn't surprise Rock to see the screen was pink. He was getting used to the pink and white world. It was almost as warm and comforting as the woman he had the urge to hold and nuzzle.

Rock had hoped to spend some time that night alone with Azzie. To talk about the business, of course. The urge to touch her, kiss her, had nothing to do with the disappointment he felt when she said goodnight and climbed up to her sleeping loft.

===#==#===

Sunday morning and it was still snowing, but the only thing Rock missed about New York was the proliferation of coffee houses. He desperately needed a caffeine fix.

"You want marshmallows in your hot chocolate?" Azzie asked, her rosy cheeks dimpling with her smile.

"I need caffeine. How about a nice cup of java strong enough to stand up a spoon in it?" The urge to growl rattled around in his chest.

"Sorry. I don't do caffeine, except what is in chocolate," she shrugged as she poured milk into a pan. "If you don't want chocolate I have some nice veggie juice."

"No, thank you," he shuddered. He enjoyed a healthy diet, but he drew the line at vegetable juice. In fact, he drew the line at most vegetables. "I really need a latte with a double shot of espresso."

"Sorry, sweetie, the closest Starbucks is over a hundred miles away."

"You're sure you don't have anything with caffeine in it? Doesn't your cousin drink coffee?"

She shook her head and his cranium rattled in response, ready to explode. No caffeine and the snow continued to fall. Did it ever do anything else in Maine? They got snow in Manhattan. A pretty little dusting in Central Park always excited the kids, but nothing like this. The snow outside was higher than Meggie and he began to worry that if it kept snowing. The shed they were staying in would be buried or collapse under the weight.

Even Meggie was getting cabin fever, and she didn't drink coffee. When Azzie wasn't keeping the child occupied, Meghan sat in the cozy little nook area playing with an old rag doll or with her tiny chin in her hands watching the snow come down thick and blowing hard. When Rock joined her at the window he could no longer see the snow family they had built Saturday morning.

===#==#===

He had shoveled the paths four times on Saturday, and twice before noon on Sunday. Once again he pulled the red cap over his ears as he looked into the white sky looking for a streak of blue that wasn't there.

The snowballs Azure hurled at him had carried a wallop. The damn woman would make a fine pitcher for the Yankees. God knows they could use one.

Meghan had loved making snow angels for the first time, but after about the hundredth one he grew tired of lifting her out of her imprint.

It had been fun.

Yesterday.

But when Sunday arrived and according to the clock it was afternoon, and the damn snow was still falling, he became itchy. He was worried about not getting back to the city and his office. There was no sign of a train anywhere in sight to take him and Meghan back to civilization. He was Rockford Hollister and he had a business to run. He was expected back in his office bright and early Monday morning, but it didn't look like he was going to make it.

Meghan had to be returned to her mother. Leaving the nanny behind had been a calamity at the time, but it had worked out well for him. It had meant he was able to spend time with Azure. Luckily the woman was good with kids, since he was useless with his daughter. It hadn't taken Rock long to realize it was all the junk food he had fed Meggie that had made her sick on the train. The nanny would never have allowed her to eat all that junk and this brief idle would never have happened.

The nanny was new, but she had a gleam in her eye whenever he arrived alone to visit with his daughter. He prided himself on keeping in shape and he knew he wasn't ugly, but he was sure the nanny saw him as a means to escape the work force. If he were ever to remarry he wanted someone who wanted him and not just a free ride.

In spite of his pounding caffeine headache and grouchy mood, Rock was glad to have had this time with his daughter. He had never seen her as an individual with thoughts or a personality before this weekend. She had always been shy with him.

He was amazed to find he had been enjoying all his time with Meghan, especially once she stopped barfing on him.

Then there was Azzie with all her delightful curves and caring attitude.

Several times Rock had tried to casually lead their discussions around to the park and the adjacent undeveloped land. Azzie spoke candidly, but didn't give too much away. He admired the loyalty she had to both her grandfather and the park, but he needed the damn information.

No matter how wonderful the time had been, this was turning into a wasted weekend. Azure Brown avoided most of his conversational gambits regarding the park, she didn't have any current music, and her wardrobe seemed to consist of fuzzy sleep pants and college tee-shirts. It didn't look like she owned anything with any sex appeal to it, but just the sound of her voice was enough to give him a woody it was getting harder and harder to conceal.

Rock decided he had all the information he needed for a takeover, courtesy of his investigators. It was time to get back to the city and put his plan in motion before his cock decided to leave Azzie's land alone. He didn't make business decisions based on boners.

Saturday night had been another night of no sleep. He had moved up to the second loft. The feather mattress she had in the "guest" loft was surprisingly comfortable, but knowing she slept in the opposite loft, separated from him by a couple of sheer curtains and a few feet or air, kept him awake late into the night. He couldn't remember any woman affecting him like this, or even making him this hard just by her presence. Other than a few accidental brushes, he hadn't touched her. He had been fighting himself and his own urges to hold her and kiss her all weekend.

He needed relief.

He needed distance.

He needed to get laid.

But not by Azure. He didn't do business that way. A little flirting to get information was acceptable, but anything more than that was despicable. Besides that, she was much too wholesome. She baked, she knitted, she raised chickens. She was not the kind of woman who could handle casual sex and he wasn't the kind of man who appreciated fresh faced country girls. Hell, when it came time to sign the contracts, her eyes would be wide open and she would know who he really was. She would turn bitter about all the wonderful sex they had had. He didn't need the recriminations. So he wasn't going to "do" her.

Everything about her screamed white picket fences and station wagons, not high rise glass and steel structures or showing off her curves in a string bikini in the Caribbean.

He would really like to see her in a string bikini. He would undo the bows with his teeth . . .

Rock shoveled the path with a vengeance. Meggie and Azure went back inside with the promise of baking brownies speeding Meggie in when she wanted to stay outside, frozen nose and all. The woman was always cooking. No wonder she packed a few extra pounds. Man! Those pounds looked good on her. They made her look warm and cuddly, not like someone who would break if you squeezed her too tight.

Meggie turned back on the path. Her eyes sparkled from the brisk air. "Daddy, is Santa going to bring my presents here?" It didn't take the little munchkin long to learn how to make and throw snowballs. She, at least, was enjoying every moment of their sojourn in the wild.

"There are still a couple of weeks before it's time for Santa. Mommy will be home by then," Rock replied.

"Ohhh!" He was a lousy father; he hated seeing the disappointment on the child's face. He wanted to run to Time's Square and buy her every doll in the Toys R Us store. Even though Rock now realized the excess of rides and sugar treats on Friday was what had made her sick and stranded them here, he'd still give her anything she wanted. He would take her on the Ferris wheel at Toys R Us as many times as she wanted, or until she turned green. On second thought, he couldn't deal with her turning green unless Azure was there to take care of the child.

He wondered if Azure had ever been to Times Square. She would probably love to see the revival of *Pippin* on Broadway, or maybe *Mamma Mia*. She did have a lot of musicals on her computer.

He should invite her to visit for New Year's Eve. He'd set her up with a nice suite at the Hyatt near Bryant Park. It had kitchenettes in the suites so she would feel at home. It wasn't as swanky as his women usually liked, but it was a nice centralized location, convenient to everything. He could stay there with her so she wouldn't feel alone and lost in the big city.

Yeah, the Hyatt was the way to go. Not too fancy to intimidate the small town girl, but still better than having her invade his place.

There are so many things we have to do to get ready for Christmas. Would you like to make ornaments today?" Azzie asked.

"Can we eat them?" Meggie asked.

"No, silly. Ornaments are decorations to hang on the Christmas tree." There was that damn smile again, so sweet, so seductive, without even a hint of come-hither in it. Rock wanted to carry her off to her loft—or the nearest snow bank—as soon as he could and devour her with passion.

Where was this coming from? Yeah, Azure was attractive in a small town girl kind of way, nothing like the models and starlets he usually partied with. Rock had to remind himself he was here on undercover business, not under-the-covers.

===#==#===

The power had come back on briefly, but the television news was filled with stories of people stranded in their vehicles and others trapped in their dark homes as a result of the downed lines and fried transmitters. Ashley had gotten into the first elevator that stopped at her floor and descended into the chaos of the lobby. She hadn't changed her clothing or brushed her hair, but since she hadn't slept, she knew her hair and makeup might be a little faded, but still impeccable.

She waited for the doorman's attention for almost thirty minutes and when the man finally focused his attention on her he refused to get her a taxi.

"I am sorry, Miss Briggs, but there are no taxi's allowed on the road today. Only emergency vehicles," the man said with lowered eyes.

"Don't be ridiculous. This is New York City. The city that never sleeps. Our cabbies drive through everything, twenty-four/seven." Her Versace boots elevated Ashley to a point where she found herself staring at the man's bald spot on the crown of his head. "I am out of food and my apartment is cold. The gas fireplace is inadequate to use as heat. I must get to the Mandarin Oriental immediately."

"I am sorry, Miss. The only way to get around the city is to walk, cross country ski, or use a snowmobile. Even if the drivers wanted to be on the roads the police are strictly enforcing the ban."

The man was condescending and obstructive. She looked at his name tag. When this was all over she would have his job.

"If you would like, you may stay down here, but it is very drafty. Mister Mosley, the concierge, is requesting all tenants stay in the apartment until we receive the all clear from the mayor."

"It's very cold up there. I don't want to be here, I want to go to Columbus Circle." If her feet weren't so cold she would have stomped one, but she was afraid a heel would break off.

"Miss Briggs, Mister Mosley really feels that you will be much safer in your own home. Con-Ed is warning of more outages. If you will return to your own apartment we will find you some food," Sahid the door man assured her.

"It is too cold to remain up there," Ashley said again.

"Have you closed all your drapes and doors to rooms you are not using? That will help to hold the heat in the room," Sahid asked.

"I do not have drapes, I have silk curtains," Ashley said indignantly.

"If you would like, Ma'am, I will come up with you and hang blankets up over your windows."

"I do not live in a tenement. I will not have blankets hanging on my windows," Ashley said stiffly.

"Very well, madam, but you must return to your apartment while the elevators are still running. You wouldn't want to climb twenty-five stories in those boots."

Ashley would see that a man with his attitude lost his job. See if he'd smirk at his betters then!. She turned on her heel and marched to the elevator. She jabbed the up button.

Damn Rockford! He should have stopped by to check on her by now.

Chapter 7

Sunday night they had homemade beef stew
and biscuits for dinner, followed by strawberry
shortcake. It had been pure torture watching the
tip of Azzie's pink tongue lick the homemade
whipped cream off her upper lip. He would have
liked to have that pleasure. He wanted to take that
whipped cream and slather it on some of her more
interesting curves and slowly lick it off.

As soon as Azzie went to the sink to start
doing the dishes, Rock and his rock hard
appendage made a quick dash out the door. He
pulled on his jacket and borrowed hat and gloves,
grabbed the shovel from the corner of the small
porch and worked on the area around the house.

What the hell was the matter with him? He
never had a woman affect him this way. She
wasn't even his type. She was too sweet. Too
helpful. Too nice.

He liked women with edge.

Half an hour later, he found himself
shoveling in darkness. He could no longer see the
glow from the house windows and knew his alone

time was coming to an end. At least the cold air and work had calmed down his body.

Now all he had to do was not get another hard-on as soon as he walked through the door. He tried not to imagine her soft clad ass cheeks in his hands or rubbing up against him.

He walked in to find Azzie and Meggie cuddled up on Meggie's bed. His child was holding the old doll while Azzie read to her from Five Little Peppers. Rock had never heard of it before, but it was an old hard cover book. He settled onto the futon with a book, but he found himself listening to her soft voice instead of paying attention to the words in his book.

Meggie's eyes drifted closed and Azzie's voice faded.

Rock wasn't ready for Azzie to leave him yet. He moved to the table and picked up the deck of cards that were stored on one of the shelves and shuffled them.

"Want to play a couple of hands of poker?" He asked with a grin.

"Poker isn't really my game. I hate losing money at it." She smiled at him.

"We don't need to play for money." His unspoken suggestion made Azure blush. He didn't know women still did that, but his Azzie did it all the time.

"No poker, but I will play gin or cribbage with you."

"Gin it is," he said. He laid the cards down on the table for her to cut for the deal.

Two hours later she had won every game, except the first. If they had been playing for money she would now own his half of Hollister & Briggs.

"Where did you learn to play like that?"

"I grew up in these mountains. A good storm used to wipe out the electricity for days, sometimes weeks at a time. We used to play cards a lot on candle nights," she said with a toss of her braid over her shoulder.

"Candle nights? I like that. In my part of the city, we very rarely lost electricity, but when we did we went in search of open restaurants."

"That sounds like fun," she said.

"Not really. The city can be frightening to a child when all the lights go off. You see a monster behind every car and down every alleyway."

"Yeah, Boston can get a little creepy too," she responded.

"You must miss living in the city?" Rock picked up a card and discarded another one.

"Not at all. My job pays a pittance, but it is one of the few jobs I can find even close to my field. It's only part time and has no benefits." Azzie picked up his discard.

"I thought you worked in education. I heard teachers get paid well, you get a vacation week every two months, and the entire summer off." This was the opening Rockford had been waiting for, so why wasn't he feeling good about it?

"That would be school teachers. They have a strong union, but for the work they do, they don't paid enough, either. I'm an adjunct at a college," she said as she studied her cards.

"An adjunct?"

"I teach college students. I do the work of a professor, without the title, the tenure, or the class hours." Azure picked up a card and laid down her hand. "Gin."

"I wish I had some Tanqueray," Rock sighed at another loss.

"Sorry, the strongest thing I have to drink is some cranberry apple cider," Azzie offered.

"If you're only working part time, what do you do with your spare time?" Rock couldn't picture her spending too much of her free time hanging around in the cramped space of the tiny house.

"On the days I don't have classes I substitute in the public schools. Plus I have a couple of other projects going."

"You work another job?" Rock didn't know anyone who worked more than one job. Even his housekeeper only worked for him. She kept his penthouse clean, stocked his cabinets, and cooked meals for when he was having an at home night.

"Of course. Living in the city isn't cheap and my position at Kenmore University doesn't pay enough to cover my property taxes." Azzie shuffled and then dealt the cards for another game of gin.

"Couldn't your grandfather help?" Now she would have to answer with some of the financial information he needed.

"He did. He bought me a small piece of land." Her answer was sparse and did not provide the informational nuggets he had hoped for.

"So you own a real house in the city?" If she liked her job and had a place to live rent-free, it might make it more difficult to get her on his side. The most important thing he had learned about Azure Brown over the course of the last few days was that she was not a mercenary woman.

"We're in my real city house right now," she said with a cold smile. Rock suppressed a shiver at the loss of warmth in her brown eyes. "I own a small strip of land in Brighton. It is between four houses. Runs right through the block." She took a sip of her hot chocolate. "According to the city's zoning laws, my land is too narrow to build a house on, so I did some online research and decided to build this 'off-the-grid' home on wheels. I pay taxes on undeveloped land. I have no running water, no connection to the sewer system, and no electricity. Or at least not the electricity bills that usually accompany city living. My house runs on solar power. I have beautiful gardens, grow my own herbs and veggies, and every year I build two more houses similar to mine to sell."

"There's a market for houses this small?" Rock couldn't believe what he was hearing. The tiny, college educated woman sitting across from him grew her own food and cooked it, plus built houses. It was obvious she was proud of her accomplishments. "How do you live with no running water in the city?"

"I have several large water tanks in my truck. I come up here to my favorite fresh water spring and refill them when I need water, and I get to visit my grandfather at the same time." Azzie shifted in her seat. It was the first sign that she looked a little uncomfortable. "A couple of times I needed water and couldn't get up here and my neighbors let me fill up with water from their hoses, but the city water is gross when you usually drink fresh spring water." It was her turn to discard. "I use natural products to clean and I run the 'grey' water through a natural filtration system I built and the reclaimed water is used to irrigate my gardens. Between my recycled water and composting, very little goes to waste."

"You must be very popular with your neighbors," Rock couldn't keep the sarcastic remark in. Composting meant throwing your rotten food into a hole in the ground, didn't it?

"Actually, I am. I have taken what was a trash filled vacant lot and turned it into a blooming paradise with a cute little house to brighten up the neighborhood. I have a pretty white picket fence around the yard and it looks like the American dream in miniature." She took another sip of her drink.

"Your house is pretty. Meggie wants a dollhouse that looks just like it." Rock gulped down his hot chocolate. He had lost control of the conversation once again. He had to get it back on the financial track.

"It's my gardens which really make it look nice. When I first got the land the neighborhood kids were fascinated watching me clear all the trash out of the lot. I saved a lot of stuff, like old bike parts, to use in the gardens. Eventually some of the kids came in to help." Azzie's smile was back. Rock really liked the way her entire face became animated when she talked about the kids.

"How long did that last?" he asked.

"All summer," she chuckled. "When I started the garden I had half a dozen kids ranging in age from four to twelve helping me to dig and turn the earth over. I taught them what wild flowers would produce pretty flowers and how to take care of them. We planted herbs and vegetables."

"The garden must have been quite impressive." He hoped he didn't sound as snarky as he felt.

"It was. When the plants were ready to be harvested, I invited them and their families over for a pot luck. For some of them it was the first time they had ever eaten any organic food. The next spring I gave them seeds and seedlings to start their own gardens in their yards. Their parents are very happy to see them cleaning up the yards and taking pride in their little patches. They've even started their own composting and pay more attention to recycling." She paused to sip at her hot chocolate. "One mother thanked me because her son had always refused to eat asparagus until last summer when he grew his own in his garden. Now it is his favorite vegetable."

Rock threw down his cards in defeat.

Damn, she was good. How do you convince a woman who is so self-reliant to sell her family land to a developer?

Who was it that said, "Tomorrow is another day"? He would sleep on it tonight and formulate another plan of attack for tomorrow.

"Are you tired, or just tired of this game?" Azure asked.

"I'm not used to all this fresh air. I think I have to call it a night," Rock said as he stood up.

He helped her clear the table before they closed it for the night. Then they parted, each heading to their separate lofts. Rock had been tempted to take Azure into his arms to kiss her goodnight. Just a gentle, little touching of the lips. But since the mere thought had his cock jump into instant hot rod of burning passion mode, he didn't dare go near the woman.

===#==#===

Azzie tossed around on her feather mattress for the third night in a row. The first night she had been nervous letting Mr. Tall, Handsome Stranger spend the night in her no-interior-walls home. She wasn't sure if her nerves were due more to her attraction to him, or because there was a strange man in her home, with nothing but a few yards of space and sheer curtains separating them. She did wish she had gone for a ladder she could pull up into the loft with her instead of the staircase.

That worry quickly faded and was replaced by another. What if she snored in her sleep? Or passed gas? That would be so embarrassing!

It was bad enough waiting to use the composting toilet until after he went out to shovel! At first she had been afraid he would never go out and she would have to go behind a bush somewhere in the middle of the blizzard. She hadn't been looking forward to freezing her tushy off, but there were certain things a woman didn't want to do with a handsome man around, especially a handsome man she was just getting to know.

Saturday night she was exhausted and hoped she would fall asleep as soon as her head hit the pillow. Unfortunately, his smile kept her awake. His smile, his eyes, his hard body. Rock kept touching her hands, back, even her face. Sometimes she thought she had caught him looking at her mouth. Did her crooked front tooth bother him that much? Maybe she should have gotten braces when she was a teenager, like her mother wanted her too. She tried to stop smiling so much, but then he would say something so silly or outlandish that she had to smile. Maybe it wasn't the tooth—maybe she had ketchup on her face or a chocolate mustache?

His mouth was so tempting. She wanted to feel it on hers. Hell, she wanted to feel it everywhere on her! She had to stop thinking about Rock before she jumped over to his loft and jumped his bones!

Azzie thanked her lucky stars that Meggie was there. Meggie made a cute little buffer. There was no way they could have sex with a child in the tiny-little-house-with-no-privacy.

Azure wasn't sure where all the sexual thoughts were coming from. She was starting to feel like a nymphomaniac, and sex had never been that big a deal to her. She didn't normally look at a guy and think about his fuckability factor.

She turned onto her stomach and punched her pillow into submission. If she wasn't going to sleep, then she had to at least change the subject matter in her brain. She'd think about Meghan and not the little girl's oh-so-sexy dad.

It was obvious Meggie loved her daddy and her daddy loved her, but the child was lonely. It was obvious in the way the child was so grateful for the attention Azzie was giving her. The poor kid had never made cookies before, nor had she ever eaten one warm from the oven. Rock's ex sounded an awful lot like Rose, Azzie's mother.

Azzie wished she could have half an hour with Jenna to make her understand how much the child needed to be close to her mother. A good nanny, like a good grandmother, was a blessing to both mother and child, but they should never be a replacement for a living mother.

Meghan was such a sweet little girl. Azzie was glad her Pop made her teach the children's craft classes. It taught her a lot about young children. Good preparation for handling a sick little girl on a train or the neighborhood kids that were searching for more adult guidance.

Since Meghan puked her way into Azzie's life, all of her childhood dreams of having a family of her own were coming back. Today she had caught herself daydreaming that she actually had that mythical family with Rock. She had to pull herself out of that particular fantasy three different times. If the train didn't pick them up soon she was afraid she would chain him up and make him her sex slave!

At least until he had fathered four or five babies on her.

Stop thinking about that man and sex! Think about work.

If she hadn't come home to run the park for Pop, she would be preparing finals for her students in American History 101 at Kenmore University. Not the most exciting job in the world. She would prefer to be a fully tenured professor and teach more advanced history classes, but jobs like that didn't open up very often. She was luckier than most young historians in academia. The university let her teach a class on the history of trains and railroads in the Northeast and another in Museum management. Not both in the same semester, but at least she did get to teach both of them. It was a good way to keep a foot in her specialized field.

Her dream job was to be a curator of the Brownville Junction Train Museum, but there was no longer any money to procure new exhibits. They had even been forced to sell off some of the existing exhibits to keep the park open. That made a full-time curator a moot point. Sure Pop would give her the title and hire her, but it would be nepotism at its worst. She didn't need her grandfather to create a job for her, not when there were so many people in the area who could use the job more.

She had hoped to save the museum with grants, but the federal money was being given out according to the old pork system and Maine didn't have that many pig farmers in Congress. Most of the private grants were now being used for "in house" projects. And since no Brown would ever let even a tiny slice of ownership out of family hands, Brownville Junction wasn't a part of any corporation's house.

It would break the heart of the history geek in her, but now that she was running most of the show, she would sell off everything in the museum if that was what it took to keep the park open and in the family.

But Sunday night it wasn't the history geek that dreamt of making love under the hidden waterfall on Humphrey's Mountain. It was the woman who had thought she had given up the dream of having a family of her own someday soon. The faceless lover of her adolescent dreams now had a face and a name worthy of the Granite Mountains. Rock. She had to wonder if he lived up to his name.

She would certainly love to give him the chance to rock her world. It was difficult to shut down her thoughts, but eventually Azzie fell into a deep sleep.

She awoke to the sun shining through her window. She hoped Rock hadn't heard any moans from her during her salacious slumbers. It would be too humiliating if he had been privy to her dreams.

She stayed in bed for a few minutes and watched a drop of water make its way down the glass. A tear rolled down her cheek in concert with the melted drop. She knew her little family was about to dissolve along with the snow.

Reality beckoned and she wanted to chase it away with a broom.

===#==#===

The first thing Ashley planned to do once the city awakened from this nightmare was to go to the new day spa on Fifth Avenue and have the works. There was a hunky masseuse there and she wanted him to give her a deep tissue massage, and anything else she could get from him, before she had to deal with the idiots in the office.

She needed her hair and nails done, too. The weekend had been stressful, and it still wasn't over. Cell service was spotty. Power was restored to her neighborhood, but who knew how long that would last? The fools on the weather said the snow was going to be followed by a deep freeze and warned that the power was still out in most of the city.

"Have you found me a cab yet?" Ashley snarled into the phone.

"Not yet, Ma'am. Most of the streets are still closed and the taxis aren't running yet," the disembodied voice answered.

She slammed the phone down. She wanted, no she *needed*, to get to Rockford's apartment.

She had bided her time waiting out his whore mongering days. Well, she didn't plan on waiting any longer. Ashley wanted him now!

Today! She thought as she stamped her Christian Louboutin on the floor and snapped the very high heel off. She hobbled into her room and cast herself onto a chair in her shoe closet while she tried to decide on a suitable replacement. Finally she settled on a Ferragamo from last year's collection. There was no good to be accomplished by ruining another pair of good shoes.

Ashley walked back towards the entry way while she pulled her coat on. She slammed the door behind her. When the lazy doorman saw she meant business he would find her a taxi, or he would be out of a job. She was going to pound on Rockford's door until he answered and then she would toss whatever piece of trash he had shacked up with for the weekend out the door.

Rockford was hers and nobody else was going to have him ever again.

Chapter 8

Azzie pulled on her fur-lined mukluks, wool hat, and old parka before trudging through the snow to the chicken coop. The snow had stopped, but the temperatures had dropped. It didn't look like the melt would begin today. She had to check for eggs, although her girls didn't usually produce many eggs during the winter. The hens needed fresh water and food, no matter what.

None of the girls ventured out into the snow to visit with her. They were too busy enjoying the warmth their snug coop still held from the heating system she had made out of black painted soda cans. With the return of the sun today, the solar panels and the chicken's heating system should be back to full strength by tonight.

She cleaned off the solar panel on top of the coop, then strode to the panel truck she used to store supplies and which held a large freezer that didn't fit into her house. As much as she loved living close to nature, even when she was in the city she ate as close to fresh as she could. She had been raised by a grandmother who in turn had been raised by a woman who had lived through the Great Depression. They believed and taught

Azzie to also believe, that if you had less than six cans of something in the pantry you faced starvation. Her little house didn't have enough cupboard space, so Azzie cheated a little and used her panel truck as storage.

It also was handy to have it close by to tow her tiny house whenever she wanted to move it.

She needed to raid her supplies. Again. Feeding a full grown man and a small child emptied her cubbies fast and she wanted more frozen fruit for Meggie. Maybe she'd make an apple pie. Rock had enjoyed her tarts, maybe he would he like her pie as well.

The fresh air invigorated her. She was really going to miss Maine after the holidays. She loved her woods and her wild weather. The sounds of Mother Nature were preferable to the constant sounds of traffic. In the city, the noise of cars whizzing by, even if they were a couple of streets away, kept her nerves on edge. She'd much rather listen to the sound of a moose calling to his mate or a mama bear warning her babies not to stray.

She loved Boston, she really did. Especially in the spring when everything brown turned green overnight and opening day would have every Bostonian on edge until the Sox won. However, she wasn't looking forward to hooking her little house on wheels up to the truck and hauling it back to her small lot in Brighton after the holidays. She was going to miss the peace and solitude of rural Maine.

Maine was her home. She had grown up running barefoot through the woods, splashing in the rivers, learning to swim in the lake, getting her first kiss behind the mock O. K. coral. Yes, she loved Boston, but this land was her home, her heart, her heritage.

This is where she truly belonged.

She had agreed to go back to teach her spring semester class in locomotion. There were half a dozen students depending on that class to complete their degrees. While she was back in Boston, Pop and Mr. Jenkins would oversee the maintenance that needed to be completed before they reopened the park in April for Patriot's Day weekend. During April and May they would only be open to the public on the weekends and school vacation weeks. However, the park was a favorite field trip for many schools, so they would be open for private functions at least one day a week. She'd like to think the influx of cash would be enough to improve the financial health of the park, but her grandfather always insisted on charging the schools barely enough to cover payroll on those days. Pop said that having the kids leave the school building for a nice spring day of fun and fresh air was good for their brains. He was right. Children needed the fresh air, the exercise, and the chance to get rowdy without getting detention.

The students received discount passes to come back with their families during the summer. In the past, very few discount cards went unused, but in recent years only a small percentage returned with the kids. The business woman she was becoming feared they were fighting a losing battle and would have to end the field trips, as they were not cost effective. The educator refused to give up on a treat the children looked forward to every year. The children needed a fun day, plus if handled properly, there would be plenty of chances for lessons to be learned. The park was full of history.

Last year Aaron Rooney, her colleague, and for a brief time, her lover, sent some of his business students to the park armed with clipboards to do a survey. The study showed that although the kids were happy and willing to come back, it was the parents who wanted to hold out for the bigger parks with the giant rides and the stuffed television characters.

The Stuffing Station, the shop where children could make their own stuffies and fill them with the traits they desired in a best friend, had Danny the Dalmatian wandering the park and posing for pictures, but apparently dogs weren't as popular as mice.

In May, after finals, she would be back to manage the park full time. Memorial Day weekend would mark the opening week of the summer season. She already had the schedule of special events filled for the entire summer. All she had to do was get a PR campaign that would get people into the park for the vintage rides rather than the death defying ones and the high admission prices of the "big boys". It would be a great summer as long as she could keep the vultures from Hollister & Briggs from swooping in and stealing the park.

There were too many times since she came back to help Pop that she had wished she had majored in business rather than history. It would have been more practical, but since Thawe had been in law school, she didn't think it would be necessary for her to run the park. Her major goal had been to be the curator of the Brownville Junction Museum, run the local historical society, and marry a nice guy to have half a dozen kids with. All those goals had been shattered with Pops' health problems last summer.

The memory of Rock and Meggie reading together in the nook yesterday morning flashed into her mind and pushed her dour business thoughts away. Azzie tried not to think about how much she was going to miss them. In a few short days, they had both wormed their way into her heart and resurrected her dreams of a family of her own.

Rock didn't talk about himself, he just said he was a businessman and left it at that, but he had a gentle way with Meggie. And he was so damn hot!

Her house was so tiny they were constantly brushing against each other. Her nipples were in a constant state of high alert. Then there were the times when his lips got so close she thought he was about to kiss her, and in those moments she forgot there was a child there. It's a good thing he was more aware of the proprieties than she was.

===#==#===

Meghan sang every song she had ever heard while eating her breakfast. When Azzie joined her in an off-key alto, Rock burst into laughter. He had been sure that Monday morning would be a disaster with cabin fever rampaging through the three of them. Instead he found he preferred listening to his two girls singing country songs into a spatula and a wooden spoon rather than rushing off to a meeting where the only goal was to make more money.

His typical Monday mornings involved his business partner wanting to recap all the connections she had made over the weekend and how they should pursue this person in order to increase their share in the marketplace or that person for the social advantages. However, lately all Ashley wanted to discuss were her plans to take over Brownville Junction. It had become an obsession of hers.

He had been on the brink of dissolving their partnership. The only real purpose of the business was to make money. Money was not enough. He needed a challenge and wanted to help people. He had already accumulated more than he could ever use in his lifetime. Money alone was not enough incentive to continue in a partnership with Ashley. She was difficult to work with. She inserted herself into his personal life and made snide remarks about the women he dated. He could imagine how she'd dig her claws into soft, little Azzie were they ever to meet.

He suppressed a shudder.

Ashley Briggs had been a lifelong acquaintance. When she proposed they go into business together, he thought it was the perfect business arrangement. He wasn't attracted to her, so there wouldn't be any sexual drama between them.

What Rock hadn't realized until it was too late, was that Ashley was the jealous, manipulative type of person. She had hidden her attraction to him, apparently for years, and once the ink was dry on the contract, she started coming on to him. He worked hard to rebuff her gently and keep their relationship friendly, but Ashley had other ideas. She became bitchy whenever he had a date. Which, he had to admit, was often. Sometimes he dated women just to avoid Ashley. Whenever there was a void in his love life she tried to fill it.

Yes, Rockford Hollister was ready to move on. Find something to do that he really enjoyed, but first he had to complete this deal for the park. He couldn't leave Ashley in the lurch.

Apparently Ashley needed this deal to go through. She was pushing too hard for it. She had something up her sleeve—he had to find out what it was before she used whatever she had to hurt Azzie. He could deal with a partner trying to jump his bones, but not one who was keeping important facts from him, and certainly not one who wanted to hurt Azzie.

He hoped the Brownville project would be so big he'd never have to see Ashley. Someone would have to be on site to ensure a smooth beginning. Whether the project turned into a failure or it was a wild success, it would be the final episode of their partnership.

He brushed aside his dark thoughts of work. It was nice to be in the borrowed flannel shirt and worn out jeans—they were comfortable. It was lucky he and Thawe were the same size. He hoped Azzie was being honest and they belonged to her cousin and not her lover. A woman who liked to take care of others and cooked like Azzie had to have a lover. What man in his right mind wouldn't want to come home and squeeze her ass?

Another homemade country breakfast filled his belly, much more satisfying than the bagel and luke-warm coffee he usually guzzled at his desk. He'd have to go out soon and shovel the paths. Meggie was wrapped up in one of Azzie's aprons and standing on a chair at the counter "helping" Azure make a pie. It looked like she was more nuisance than help, but Azure was an angel and never let them see any frustration she may have felt. Instead of the horrified shrieks he heard whenever Ashley encountered Meggie, there was a lot of giggling going on.

"Even with the snow stopping, the train may not make it here today. They'll have to clear out a lot of snow before they can get into the utility buildings, and they have to get into the utility buildings before they get the tracks cleaned to come out here. I'm afraid we're not top priority." Azzie's concerned voice interrupted Rock's thoughts.

"Are you that anxious to get rid of us?" His voice sounded gruff, even to himself.

"Not at all. I'm enjoying the company. I just thought you might be getting sick of my cooking." Azzie smiled at him.

Rock wanted to brush the streak of flour off her cheek, dig his fingers into her hair, nuzzle her neck. He jumped to his feet. "I don't believe I could ever get sick of your cooking." Heat rushed to his face like a flash fire running down a gas line. He had better not be blushing. He was a cool, suave player. He didn't blush, especially not in front of a country bumpkin. "I'd better go open up those paths again. Don't want your chickens to have to wait for their fresh water." He grinned. If he didn't get out and breathe the cold air, he would end up backing the poor woman into a corner and kissing her as silly as he was feeling.

When he reentered the house, the first thing he saw was his daughter with peanut butter smeared all over her face.

"What are you girls up to?"

"We's making bird feeders," Meggie mumbled around her finger.

"Really?"

"Yup. Azzie runned out of suey and we need to give the birds some fat to help them keep warm," Meggie shared her knowledge happily.

"Suey?"

"Suet. I ran out of suet and we are using pine cones I had gathered earlier this fall. We're coating them with peanut butter and bird seeds."

Azzie smiled as she stuck her finger full of peanut butter into her mouth.

Rock grew hard just watching her suck on her finger.

"I have to go out and widen the path to the tracks," he practically stammered as he turned and rushed back out the door.

===#==#===

The next morning, Rock was still sitting at the table drinking some fancy fruit tea. It wasn't the coffee he had been jonesing for, but the edge seemed to be off of his caffeine craving and the tea was actually quite nice. A bit on the sweet side, not harsh and bitter like the espresso he usually drank in the morning, but a refreshing change.

Azzie was at the tiny sink washing dishes by hand. Until this weekend he had never imagined any young woman washing dishes by hand, but Azzie said it was the way she liked to do them. Her hair was gathered into a ponytail that swished with her movements. Rock wanted to release her hair and bury his face in it. Her fuzzy pajama bottoms clung low on her hips. His hands itched to run over her backside to see if the pants were as soft as they looked and her buttocks as firm. Even though he never missed a day in the office, he couldn't deny that his stay in this overgrown shed and the close proximity to this sexy woman was doing randy things to his libido.

He was even turned on by her wide collection of fleece pajama bottoms, even the green ones with Rudolph and his red nose on them.

Rockford Hollister liked being Rock, the man who shoveled snow and snuggled his daughter. The time he was spending with Azzie and his little girl was the best thing that had happened to him. He felt some strange emotion, he couldn't put a name to, but he wanted the feeling to continue. He had never felt this way in New York, not even at his houses in the Hamptons or Palm Beach.

He felt complete. Content and complete.

===#==#===

Ashley picked up the cordless phone from the couch cushion next to her. She punched in the speed dial and admired her new manicure. Her nails were all dressed up with no place to go. The line rang once. Twice.

"Hallo?" the woman on the other end sounded like she had just run up the side of the Empire State Building.

"Let me speak to Rockford," Ashley demanded.

"I am very sorry, Meiss Briggs, but Meester Rock, he is not at home dis evening," the woman replied in her singsong voice.

"It is imperative that I speak to him. Where is he?" Ashley's temper was rising. She didn't like talking to the help, especially this woman.

"Dat I do not know. Meiss Jenna left de little one with Meester Rock before de big snow. Den he say he will take de li'le girl out and dat I can have de weekend off." Ashley could hear the insolence in the woman's voice. "I vesit my dotter at de college and I stayed wit her until it was safe to come home. I 'ave not seen Meester Rock since las' Tursday. I do not know where dey is."

Ashley slammed down the phone.

The woman was lying to her. There was no way Rockford would have that kid all this time. He might have fathered the little brat, but there was no way he could take care of her. He knew less about kids than she did, and Ashley was pleased to admit that she knew nothing at all.

Rockford should have listened to her three years ago when she tried to tell him not to hire that woman. Mrs. Mogambo couldn't handle simple phone calls and she always had a bad attitude when she spoke to Ashley. She hated to think of how the woman talked to major clients when they called.

The next time she spoke to Rockford she would make it clear the woman had to go.

Chapter 9

By mid-morning of the fourth day, Rock knew his time in the little house was coming to an end. He wasn't ready to leave.

Azure went out to start up the JIC to recharge the golf cart batteries that supplied the tiny house with power. Rock and Meggie once again shoveled the paths. His back, shoulders, and arms protested at the extensive work-out and he was sweating like a Knicks forward, but he found the repetitive work in the pine scented air refreshed his brain cells. He hadn't thought so clearly in years.

After a thorough, but quick, shower in the miniscule bathroom, he dressed in his own clean jeans and the flannel shirt belonging to her cousin. The shower had to be short and sweet, due to the water situation, but it made him more appreciative of the necessities of life. He would have to rethink the water usage in his homes when he returned to civilization, because as Azzie pointed out, water was a valuable resource and needed to be conserved and protected.

Rock was grateful to sit at the at the small kitchen table sipping hot chocolate with Meggie perched on his knee while Azure continued to read them the story of The Five Little Peppers. It was a quiet and peaceful break from the hectic life he led in New York City. A life he should be anxious to get back to, but found himself strangely reluctant to reenter.

A knock at the door startled them all, causing Rock to spill hot chocolate over his hand. A foul curse erupted from his mouth.

"Daddy, you said a bad word," Meggie stage whispered in his ear.

"I know, sweetheart. I'm sorry," he whispered back. "I shouldn't have said it."

Rock glared at the door as Azure opened it with a beaming smile on her face. This could only mean the train was running and their time together was over. Was Azzie that happy to be rid of them that her entire face glowed?

"Hey, Azzie, your grandfather sent the number nine out for you as soon as we were able to get the tracks cleared. There's been a lot of damage and he needs you to come in," the brawny young man said.

"Are the roads cleared?" Rock asked.

The young man shook took off his wool cap and knocked his boots against the step before he entered the house.

"Come on in and close the door, Bobby. Have some cocoa while we get ready," Azzie said as she walked over to the stove.

"The roads leading into town and the highway are slow, but drivable," the young man answered Rock's question as he closed the door. "Side roads don't exist and probably won't for another few days."

The urge to punch the guy in the face boiled inside of Rock as the guy stared at Azure's ass as she moved around.

"Is it your Granny's special recipe?" Bobby asked as he kicked off his boots.

Azzie poured the promised treat into a mug and placed it in front of Bobby. "Would I dare to make it any other way?"

He chuckled. "No, I can see your Granny now, coming down from heaven with her hands on her hips and cussing you out for using 'that nasty store bought, powdered stuff'."

Azure laughed along with *Bobby* as she reached for the tins she had stored the cookies and brownies in. She put them into a canvas Brownville Junction tote bag. Then she put the ornaments she and Meggie had made into another canvas tote.

Why is she bagging everything? Rock thought.

"Meggie, you can take these ornaments home with you for your tree," Azure said in a voice that sounded a bit too bright and cheery for Rock's taste. Was she really that happy to get rid of her unwelcome guests? She hadn't seemed to mind having them here before *Bobby* showed up.

"Daddy, we needs a tree? I wanna pink one like Azzie's."

"Of course, sweetheart. We'll get one when we get home, but I think it will be green."

"You know, the local Boy Scout troop sells trees at our gate. You won't find any trees better 'an ours," Bobby said. "And the troop can really use the support."

"We're driving back to New York City." Rock didn't like this guy at all.

"That's fine. You can pick out a nice full tree and the boys 'ill tie it up on your roof all nice and tight," *Bobby* assured him.

"Oh, Daddy! Please!" Rock couldn't say no to the little girl dancing in front of him. She was so excited about getting the tree that she hadn't realized they would be leaving Azzie behind. He hated to think of the tears he was in for then.

Once they were dressed in their outdoor clothes, they walked down the path Rock had shoveled earlier. Meggie skipped in excitement at the thought of riding on the train. Her fear of being sick replaced by the sense of adventure Azure had imparted with all the train stories she had related to the child all weekend. Another thing he was grateful to Azzie for.

When they arrived at the depot, Azzie squatted in front of Meggie. "Sweetie, would you like to help the engineer drive the train?"

His daughter's face lit up. "Yes. Yes. Yes."

"Won't it be crowded with all of us in the engine?" His voice was laced with sarcasm.

"It would be if we were all to ride in it, but I thought we would let Meggie help drive the train while you and I sat in the passenger car and enjoyed the ride."

He felt like a lout for unleashing his sarcasm on Azzie. For the first time since he had met her, she sounded hesitant when she answered his question. She had been nothing but kindness and he had thought she was trying to avoid riding the train alone with him and Meggie. Now it looked like she had been trying to set it up so the two of them could be alone for the short trip. They had never been alone together. Was she trying to get a date out of him? He hoped so.

He'd be more than happy to oblige. There were so many places in New York he had thought of taking her with each shovel of snow he hoisted. He probably wouldn't be able to get her out of this dump before the holidays. Once the Browns agreed to sell the place to him, or he completed his hostile takeover, he knew Azzie would insist on completing the holiday season. She'd want to do it for all the children that looked forward to coming to Brownville Junction to see Santa. He'd give her that time. But he wanted her in the Big Apple for New Year's Eve.

The train ride through the winter wonderland was uneventful and too short. Rock had actually become tongue-tied while she spent the time pointing out the snow-covered sights. She didn't ask him for a date, and he couldn't come up with the right words.

He had suddenly found a conscience, and it was very inconvenient. He couldn't tell her about the take-over yet and he couldn't ask her out without telling her first. She had a right to know.

When the train stopped at the station, he wasn't ready to part with Azure. The next time they met she would know he was the infamous "looter" trying to "steal" Brownville Junction.

He dreaded seeing the look on her pretty face when she found out the truth. He watched as she viewed her world through the train's windows. Rock felt as if he had been struck by lightning when he realized she truly loved this wilderness.

Meggie was as reluctant to leave her new friend as he was. When they were reunited, she asked if they could go to the museum with Azzie to see "Big Henry". Rock jumped at the opportunity to postpone their goodbyes. He didn't understand why, but he knew he wasn't ready to have his sojourn in the wilds of Maine come to an end.

Rock wanted, needed, more time with this woman before she found out he was Rockford Hollister. He knew Azure would be angry for a while, but then her good sense would tell her it was time to act like an adult and not a spoiled little girl not getting her way. She was a gentle, loving woman. She would forgive him for any wrongs she thought he had committed. Then she would want to see him, be with him.

She had to. She was a woman and women always forgave him. But Azure Brown was unlike any other woman he had ever met.

Rock hoped her good sense would kick in. He hated the thought of having to start all over again with her, but he would if he had to.

She was the one woman he could not let get away.

Chapter 10

"Humphrey Brown arrived in the new world on a convict boat. He had been convicted of disrespecting an Earl and was sent to a logging enterprise in the New Hampshire territory," Azure spoke in a tour guide voice. "Family lore has it that the Earl was Humphrey's half-brother. I spent the better part of my sophomore spring semester in England trying to confirm it. I couldn't find enough evidence either way, but it would explain a lot about the man."

"So he didn't come over on the Mayflower?" Rock joked. "I thought all you New Englanders were descended from the Puritans."

"Far from it," Azure chuckled. "Humphrey came over long before those prissy panted interlopers even thought about venturing out into the world. Of course, he didn't have much choice in the matter." She shrugged her shoulders and moved on to the next exhibit. "Not being a man who liked to take orders, especially at the end of a whip, he escaped into the woods not long after he arrived. Eventually he wandered into a Penobscot encampment and saved a young child from drowning. Luckily for him, the child was the chief's son."

"Who were the Penobscots?" Meggie asked.

"The Penobscots were the indigenous people of Maine." Azzie saw the confusion in Meggie's eyes she went on to clarify, "The Natives, or as Columbus and his crew called them, 'Indians'. Humphrey's story is not recorded in the official history of the Confederacy of the People, but it has been handed down throughout our family history.

"The chief didn't have any single daughters to give to Humphrey, so as a reward, Humphrey was given one of the shaman's daughters. When the tribe moved into this area to escape the loggers' cruelty and attempts to enslave or exterminate them, Humphrey claimed the lake and the mountains surrounding it as his land. By this time he was considered a friend of the People and they, the Penobscots, allowed it, even though their own beliefs didn't allow for one man to own the earth."

She stopped in front of an old map. "Throughout the generations the family has managed to retain possession. Even when the mighty white rulers in England handed out large land grants, the family somehow managed to retain the land. We've lost sections here and there," she pointed to a few areas on the map, "some were sold off. We lost other bits to the government, but we've always managed to retain this section. We'll never sell it, even though there are always scoundrels trying to get it away from us. They'll never be able to. The great grandmother of us all foresaw the greed of the interlopers. She had powerful magick in her. The Great Grandmother put a blessing and a curse on our land," Azzie was a natural storyteller. Rock could see the awe on his daughter's face.

Rock couldn't imagine a family owning the property for that many centuries, except for the landed gentry in Europe, and even they had gone through bad times where they had lost extensive tracts of land. Most of the properties of the early settlers were not in family hands anymore—either the families had moved on or they were National Historic sites.

"What do you mean by a blessing and a curse?"

"As long as we care for the land, it will always be ours, but if we allow the land to go to an outsider, all hell will break out on our family and on anyone connected with taking our land." Azzie shrugged her shoulders. "Pop says our current problems are due to my mother and uncle leaving the land. They want to sell it so they can have oodles of money to roll around in and live a jet set life."

"A jet set life sounds exciting. Wouldn't you like to have that kind of money?" His chest tightened as he awaited her answer.

"It would be nice to see ancient antiquities, I'd love to visit the great museums, but I'm not a party girl. I don't have to be seen in the best restaurants, drink the most expensive champagne, date the wealthiest men," she sent him a dazzling smile. "I am content with my world the way it is. Once I get this park back on the right track I will be able to leave someone else in charge occasionally while I get to see places like the Acropolis, The Coliseum, The Pyramids, the Outback."

"The Outback," he choked. She had mentioned the entire world, except for New York City.

"I heard there are a lot of really hot men in the Outback. What red blooded, single woman wouldn't have that on her bucket list?"

"Wouldn't you enjoy a life of ease, living in a bigger house?" Rock asked. He didn't understand the little ache in his belly while he waited for her answer or the pang of jealousy he felt when she talked about Australian men.

"I am happy with my little house. It leaves a tiny footprint upon the earth. It keeps me close to nature, even when I live in the city." She gave him a wry smile. "I could live in a big house if I wanted to. My Pops offered to set me up when I moved to Boston. He would have bought me a mansion if that is what it took to make me happy. But there is too much of that barefoot child that slept most of the year in her tree house in me to be happy in a McMansion. Besides, a big house means a lot more housework and I really hate cleaning."

"Wow! You slept in a tree house?" At Azure's nod, Meggie turned a bright smile on her father. "Daddy, can we sleep in Azzie's tree house?"

"I'm sorry, honey, but there is much too much snow and it is way too cold." Gratitude swamped him as Azure saved him from having to break his daughter's heart. He and his beautiful little girl had become close this weekend and he liked having his child's love. He hadn't realized what he had been missing out on by not spending more time with her, but now that he did he never wanted to be without her again.

"Can we come back when the snow is gone and sleep in the tree house?" Meghan lifted glowing eyes to Azure.

Rock also turned his eyes on her. "It's up to your daddy," Azure said. "You are both welcome back here anytime."

Meggie squealed and threw her arms around her new friend's legs. "Thank you, Azzie! We'll come back tomorrow!"

"Sweetie, the snow is going to be here for a long time. Several months, at least, because it is winter and this is Maine. You would have to wait until June or July, summertime." Azzie bent down and cuddled the disappointed child next to her chest.

"Daddy, I don't wanna go home. I wanna stay here with Azzie!" Meggie cried.

"I know, baby, but we have to go home so you can see your mother." Rock understood where his daughter was coming from. He wanted to stay with Azure longer too. She had a way of making them both feel comfortable, like they were all part of the family.

"Would you like to hear some more about the railroad or are you ready to find your car?"

Meghan pulled out of Azure's arms and grabbed Rock's hand. "More story, please."

"Okay. Here we go. Thousands and thousands of our trees were harvested in order to supply the lumber for the railroad ties, the wooden planks that go between the metal rails. We supplied the wood for most of the railroads this side of the Mississippi."

"Impressive," Rock mumbled.

"It is ironic that old Humphrey was sent here as a logger and he ran off to create our dynasty and three hundred years later our family made a fortune selling our trees."

Oh, dear, she thought, *I delve deep into my favorite subject and bore the stuffing out of him. Too bad it's not his pants.* Azzie had to suppress the giggle that wanted to spring out of her mouth. She was an adult woman, an adjunct college professor, she didn't do girlish giggles.

"This is Big Hank," she said, running her hand over the nose of a pristine steam engine. "In 1843 this handsome hunk of metal was the first engine to make the run from Boston to Old Orchard Beach, Maine."

"That would make Big Hank about one-hundred and seventy years old," Rock sounded doubtful. "He looks extraordinarily good for his age."

"We have a video presentation with the original newspaper sketches, tintypes taken in 1856, pictures of Big Hank when my great-grandfather bought him, and tons of pictures and videos of my great-grandfather and Pop restoring Old Hank to his former glory. It was a major enterprise, but Hank is our pride and joy. He gets to rule the rails every Patriot's Day and Fourth of July."

"Patriot's Day? Isn't that some strange holiday only celebrated in Boston and everyone runs in the Marathon?" Rock asked.

"Since we were once a part of Massachusetts, we still celebrate the holiday. Mainers like their traditions and their days off." Azure's smile warmed Rock in places he didn't want to be warmed in front of his daughter. He would love to get this woman alone for a weekend. A very long weekend.

To get his mind off all the erotic things he wanted to do to Azure, Rock ran his fingers over the detailing on the engine. "Is this copper of bronze?"

"Good eye." She ran her delicate, but very capable, finger over the same details. "This is copper." She ran her finger over another part of the detail. "This is bronze, and this part here is brass. The locomotive is made out of cast iron."

"It must be valuable," Rock said with a frown.

"Every few years some museum or other will offer us a small fortune for Hank," Azzie said. "Recently a Japanese company offered us twice as much as our previous highest offer."

"So if you sold this engine you could pay off all debts, upgrade equipment, get new rides?" His jaw looked hard.

"There is nothing wrong with our rides or equipment. Our park gives our visitors a glimpse of life in the old days. You walk down our Main Street and you expect to see Judy Garland singing about Harvey girls, or Robert Preston marching a band with seventy-six trombones toward the town center. We remind people of a time when neighbors knew each other and kids played out in the streets." She felt tears flooding her eyes. "We'll never sell Big Hank. He's the heart and soul of Brownville Junction. He's pulled trains here since Patriot's Day 1946 and he hasn't missed a year since."

"But . . ."

"Never!" She turned her back and walked out of the museum.

What had just happened? Azzie looked devastated and Rock didn't know why.

Chapter 11

Fury shook Rock to his core when he realized he had to leave Brownville Junction without seeing Azure again. He had planned on giving her a kiss to remember him by. Instead, when he carried Meggie out of the museum to look for Azzie, *Bobby* had been waiting for him with new clothes, all with the Brownville Junction logo on them and directions on where to go to retrieve his car. Someone had shoveled him out so there would be no further delay to his departure.

When he and Maggie exited the employees lounge in their new clean clothes, Rock asked several employees where he could find Azzie. They all shook their heads and walked away until *Bobby* grinned at him and waved his hand in a circle, saying, "Around."

Though they didn't see Azzie, she had made sure they were prepared for the road. After Rock had buckled Meggie into her car seat, he stood up to find a couple of teenagers with their arms loaded down with supplies standing next to him.

"Azzie asked us to bring you these things for your trip home," the redheaded boy said.

"We should be okay," Rock had replied.

"Azzie says you're flatlanders and you are woefully unprepared for driving the roads in these conditions." The redhead was not taking no for an answer.

Rockford had his pride, and the thought that Azzie saw him as incapable of navigating the roads hurt.

"I'm sure we'll be fine."

"The news says road conditions are pretty bleak. If you would like to wait for them to improve, we can fix you up with a room at either the bed and breakfast or the hotel. No problem," the young man spoke again.

"We really have to get home. I'm sure we'll be fine once we reach the interstate," Rock said firmly.

"Okay, but first we have to ask you to take the little girl out of the car for a few minutes. Bruce is on his way. He's coming to put some chains on your tires."

"That isn't necessary. I have all weather tires on the car." Rock couldn't believe Azzie thought so little of his ability to drive through the streets she was sending him chains.

"Sorry, mister," the boy chuckled. "No matter how good your tires are, you're gonna need the chains, even on all weather tires. Bruce will be here in a couple of minutes with his jack and the chains. It won't take long," the redhead continued. "If you don't let us put the chains on, Ms. Brown will have our jobs."

"I can't believe Azzie would fire you just because I said no." That wasn't the soft hearted woman who took in strangers during a blizzard. That woman would never hold an employee responsible for a choice another person made.

The redhead's face showed his horror. "Azzie is really nice, but she is still Ms. Brown, and she says safety is our number one priority. If we let you go off without the proper equipment to ensure your safety and that of your little girl, we will be fired. Ms. Brown doesn't fool around with stuff like that, even if Azzie feels bad about it."

"What's all that stuff you're carrying?" Rock still couldn't see Azzie as a hard ass task master. So he asked the question that had been bugging him since the young men had walked up to him.

"We have a couple of pillows, blankets, and two sleeping bags, just in case you have to pull over somewhere along the road."

"I'm sure we'll be fine," Rock said.

"Those are the most famous of flatlander words. Usually when we hear them we alert rescue to stand by," the kid smirked at Rock. "We also have a bunch of sandwiches, fruit, and some goodies in the cooler, along with individual milk and juice bottles. The news reports say most of the store shelves are empty." The boy shrugged his shoulders. "It happens every time the weather guys predict a storm. You go to the store and there's no milk, bread, or batteries anywhere."

"It's been several days since the storm began, I'm sure the stores have received shipments since then." Rock wanted this foolish conversation to end so he could get the hell out of there. If Azzie didn't want to stop by and wish them a safe trip, so be it. He wanted to get on the road and get out of Maine's backwoods.

"We also brought a couple of thermoses with hot chocolate and coffee. Azzie said you like your coffee high-test, so it's black and unsweetened."

"Yeah, but I threw a lot of sugar packets in the condiment bag," the dark haired boy said as he opened the other back door.

Rock was willing to bet his entire net worth that if Azure Brown had been a stranded motorist, her car would be filled with the things needed to survive anything from a zombie attack to a nuclear holocaust. "Is the hot chocolate Azzie's grandmother's secret recipe?" Rock couldn't resist asking.

"Sorry," the young man shook his head, "I wish it was, but it's from the commissary so it's your typical chocolate drink."

"Please tell Azzie that I'm grateful for her generosity and thoughtfulness, but I'm sure we'll be fine once we get moving."

"Mister, I think you're making a big mistake. The roads are crap and the rooms here are warm and clean. You should really stay here for another day or two," the other kid said as he walked around the car. He had been holding onto the back fender when his feet came go out from under him on the icy snow and he fell splat on the ground.

"And that is why you're not on the hockey team, Francis. You can't stay on your feet long enough to get to center ice," the redhead laughed at his friend. Then his face grew more sober. "He's right. The roads really are crappy. You should stick around another day or two and let the plows and sanders do their thing."

"Thank you, but we'll be fine."

Bruce arrived a few minutes later and popped the chains onto each wheel as if it was nothing. Then to add insult to Rock's injured pride, the bearded giant handed him half a dozen flares. "Just in case."

They hadn't left the parking lot before his vehicle had fishtailed several times, but he was determined to get on the road. It wasn't very long before Rock realized the two boys knew what they were talking about. He might have turned back if more than the center of the road had a path plowed. It was barely big enough for his car to drive down; there certainly was not enough room for him to make a three point turn, especially for his Escalade.

He had assured himself that the major highways would be in better shape—he hadn't realized the hours of driving he had before he ever reached a major highway. He had been overly optimistic to think he might make it home to New York City in one day.

He should have stayed on at Brownville Junction. Too bad the invitation to stay hadn't come in Azure's sweet voice. If she had offered to let them stay with her for a few more days he wouldn't have been able to refuse.

The rest of the day Meghan alternated between singing every song she knew at full blast, something the subdued child he knew prior to the weekend would never have done, and crying because she missed Azzie. He couldn't find the right words to soothe the poor little thing. Rock had even tried singing with her.

He wished Azure was in the car with them. She'd know what to do to cheer Meggie up. Just her presence would cheer him up.

===#==#===

Life was coming back to NYC, but still no word from Rockford. Even his secretary put down the romance novel she was reading long enough to say that she hadn't heard from "the boss" at all and admitted she was worried about him.

Whoever the little slut he had hooked up with was, Ashley planned on ripping her hair out. One clump at a time. Rockford had never missed a day's work before for any of his little club cuties, what was so special about this one that he would take off and not even bother to call in?

He should have at least called her to make sure she was okay. She needed things and wasn't around to make sure she was all right.

Ashley fumed all the way to Rockford's building. The driver seemed to think he had a tourist in the cab and drove all around the park before finally pulling up in front of the Mandarin.

It was a lovely building. As soon as Ashley had heard Rockford was buying an apartment in the building, she tried to get one there, too. Unfortunately, Rockford had done much better with his investments than she had and the price of the apartment she wanted was prohibitive.

A doorman approached the cab to open the door for her while she paid off the driver. Once again she refused to tip the imbecile. He didn't deserve the consideration after ripping her off and driving her all over the city.

Ashley climbed out of the vehicle and allowed the doorman to get a good view of her legs. He stayed on the sidewalk while she walked into the building and headed for the elevators. The concierge sat behind a desk and called out to her as she headed for the bank of elevators.

How vulgar!

"Excuse me, Miss. Everyone entering the building must check in with me."

"I'm here to see Mr. Hollister." Ashley looked down her long nose at the man.

"Mr. Hollister is not here. If you would like to leave him a message, I would be happy to see he receives it when he gets in." The man pushed a pen and paper at her.

"I'll give him my own message when he gets home. Thank you. I'm just going to go up and wait for him in his apartment." Ashley pushed the paper back to the concierge.

"I'm sorry, Madam, but you are not allowed to wait for him in his apartment. You must be on

Mr. Hollister's list before we can allow you to go upstairs unescorted."

"Really," Ashley used her droll voice, "I am a close personal friend of Rockford's in addition to being his business partner. Of course I am allowed upstairs."

"Madam, you are not on Mr. Hollister's list, so you will not be going anywhere except out the door. Lindt, please escort this woman out to the sidewalk and summon a taxi should she need one."

"How dare you speak to me in such a manner. As soon as Rockford hears of your insolence you will be out of a job," she snarled at the man behind the desk.

Another man wearing the livery of a doorman walked up to her and tried to cup her elbow. "How dare you touch me!" She wrenched her arm away, but the man still herded her to the door.

Once again ensconced in the back of a cab, Ashley decided that once she married Rockford she would insist he get rid of that ghastly apartment and find one in a building that treated her with the respect she deserved.

Chapter 12

The Big Apple had lost its shine while Rock had spent the long weekend snowbound in Maine. He had arrived Thursday to slushy streets and dour faced people, which was okay because it matched his own mood.

He had grown used to the lush green pines, the blue of the spruces, and the sparkling white of the snow. He even missed the constant bird songs that had woken him up once the snow stopped falling.

Rockford had never felt so bedraggled in his life. Not after a fraternity party, not even after the bender he went on when he found out Jenna was pregnant and refused to give their marriage another try.

The drive back to New York was an experience he didn't want to repeat any time soon. The roads were so bad that they had to stop in Portland and spend the night in a hotel near the airport there. Rock had considered trying to get a flight from there back to the city, but after a few phone calls, he was forced to realize that driving was actually his best option.

The blizzard that had kept him trapped in the tiny house in Maine had covered the entire Northeast region, closing down all the major cities and highways. Azure had been right to keep all the people still in the park at her hotel for the duration. The radio airwaves were filled with horror stories of people who had been trapped in their cars. They had sat on the highways waiting to be rescued, some within feet of their exit and not even knowing it. Most of them were woefully unprepared to be stranded on the roadside, and several had died from leaving their car running and not getting out occasionally to remove the snow from near the tailpipe.

Meggie had cried herself to sleep in the back of the car and when they arrived in his garage he couldn't bear to hear her cry for Azzie again, so instead of waking the child, he lifted her into his arms and carried her to the elevator and into his penthouse.

His penthouse felt large, cold, and foreign after three and a half days in Azzie's tiny home.

He placed Meggie on the big bed in the guest room. He had never had a room decorated for his child, he had never even thought about it before, because she had never spent a night in his home. Until now.

Tomorrow he would have Donna find him an interior decorator that specialized in children's rooms to redo this room for Meggie. He and Jenna had a lot of talking to do. He wanted joint custody and if Jenna would not agree to that, he'd go for full custody. He wanted his daughter to have a stable home and he was ready to provide that for her. He had already missed out on so much in her life, he didn't intend to miss any more of it.

After he had tucked Meggie in and he was sure she was sound asleep, Rock called the nanny to ask her to bring over some clothes for Meggie. She arrived less than an hour later and informed him that she had orders from Jenna to "retrieve the child."

It broke his heart when Meggie clung to his neck and begged him to let her stay with him. "I want to stay with you, Daddy. You and Azzie." Her tears saturated his shirt until the nanny had to finally peel his daughter out of his arms. He wanted to stop the nanny, but upon the advice of his attorney he let the child go. For now.

After they left, Rock had made himself a hot chocolate from a package his housekeeper kept in the cupboard for herself, and watched The Music Man. The version with Robert Preston and Shirley Jones in it. Azure was right, none of the powder mixes could compare with the delicious drink she served in her little home. She was also right about the movie; he could picture Professor Harold Hill singing his way down the Main Street in Brownville Junction in a red uniform while boldly leading a boys' band. Although, now the band would not be just boys, there would be girls in it, too. Otherwise the park would be sued for discrimination.

He wondered if Azzie had thought about having band competitions at the park. It would be a great way to bring in crowds, provide entertainment, and it could be done without costing the park much money. They could start small with just regional bands, but within a few years they could expand the competition.

He pulled his fancy-ass phone out of his pocket and started making notes for inexpensive ways to grow the park's visitors.

He didn't bother going back to the office on Friday. He didn't want to deal with Ashley.

He had to tell her he had changed his mind about acquiring the park.

===#==#===

The following week dragged by. After Rock had phoned the nanny, he had placed an order with a florist to send Azure a bouquet of pale pink roses in a Waterford crystal vase, along with a note telling her that he and Meggie had arrived home safely. He needed to thank her for her hospitality.

A few days later the mail brought him a stiff thank you note from Azzie for the flowers. Not a personal word was to be found in the note.

The next day he found a book on Maine history in the bookstore and had it expressed to her.

The day after that, he sent her a deck of pink playing cards and a fancy cribbage board. Within two days of each gift being sent Rock received a polite thank you note. Each note was sent to his address and only had the name Rock on it. He had never fessed up to his full name, and now he was desperately searching for a way to break the news to her. He finally decided to wait until Christmas Eve, when he would travel to Maine and confess all to her. By that time he would have taken care of everything at the office and the park would no longer be threatened.

===#==#===

A week later the phone mocked him from the center of his desk. "Why don't you ring, dammit?" The phone remained silent. "She must have received that edible arrangement I sent yesterday. I made sure the card had my number on it." The phone continued to ignore him. He had even taken the phone into the bathroom with him when he showered that morning.

Saturday Rock sent her an assortment of chocolate delights. Sunday he had a beautiful handmade pink and white quilt delivered. Monday he sent her a large box of handmade Victorian ornaments. They were all pink. As soon as he had seen them, Rock knew they had to belong to Azure. He had been afraid he might get them back in pieces, but the thank you note had a little more warmth in it, though it still could have passed as a missive from Satan's frozen heart. Today he sent her a vintage Lionel train set. He could picture it set up in her house, the tracks circling through the two lofts.

Rock hoped to see those trains running on their tracks soon. Real soon.

===#==#===

He was avoiding her and Ashley would not allow Rockford to treat her like that.

He had missed more than a week in the office and didn't give her any explanation for his absence. He just muttered something about accumulated vacation time and kept working on his computer.

He never even looked at her!

Never asked if the blizzard had hurt her in anyway.

He had changed. She didn't know how and she didn't know why, but she knew he had changed.

It was time he realized they were meant to be together. It was what he had signed up for when they became partners—he had to know the ultimate goal was not just for them to make their own fortunes, but to be together.

===#==#===

It felt like forever since Azzie had last seen Rock. He had sent her a gift every day, including Sunday, which meant it was a special deliver and cost a fortune to mail. The money involved didn't impress her, but his tenacity did. The latest package contained an antique train set. She wasn't angry at him anymore. It had taken her a few days to realize he didn't know what he had said to hurt her. She supposed because he was a man little things like feelings were a minor annoyance and not to be considered. He probably didn't even realize that to her Old Hank was more like a member of the family than just a hunk of steel that moved around on tracks.

Tonight she would call him. It was time to forgive him for his careless words. She wanted to hear his voice, see if his voice really could make her insides melt like chocolate in the hot sun. If it wasn't a trick her memory was playing on her, then she was in trouble. No one had ever made her feel like that before, not even Kevin Makem, her eight grade crush, and Kevin was the first boy to ever make her feel "those" feelings. Not that she ever had a chance to act on those feelings. Danny went steady with Linda Castile that entire year. Linda did modeling and was "discovered." She went off to become a sitcom star, leaving Danny alone in her dust trail. Unfortunately, Rebecca Moss was waiting in the wings to comfort the poor boy. Azzie never stood a chance.

With the decision to call him made, she was in the middle of cleaning the diner's grill when a big gust of wind alerted her to someone opening the door. It was snowing again, just mini-squalls, but she was afraid it was enough to keep people close to home again. They really needed a big turnout if they were ever going to bring the books into the black this year, and she wanted the books to be as black as the grill.

She looked over her shoulder in time to see Bobby walk in, stomping snow off his boots. "Yer grandpa wants to see ya in his office."

"Thanks, Bobby, I'll go over there as soon as I finish up in here." Azzie continued scrubbing the grill. She expected Bobby to leave—as the head groundskeeper he still had a lot to do to prepare for the weekend crowd.

"He said that you were to drop everything and go right over there." Bobby looked uncomfortable. "He has a woman in the office with him."

Did Bobby think her grandfather had a girlfriend? Azzie thought about it a minute. It would really surprise her if Pop did have a one, but it wouldn't bother her. Much. Her Pop was a still a vibrant man and Granny wouldn't want him to live out the rest of his life in mourning; she'd want him to have friends, to be happy. Maybe he wanted to invite his new lady friend to Christmas but he wanted Azzie to meet her first.

Azzie stripped off her work gloves and grabbed her lambskin lined jacket. She stopped in front of her Grandfather's office and smoothed down her hair before turning the knob. "Hey, Pop," she said as she walked through the arched door.

"Azure, I'd like you to join us for this meeting." Her grandfather's use of her formal name had Azzie looking up from the antique doorknob her hand rested on. He never called her anything but Azzie unless there was serious business to attend to. A woman sat at the desk in front of Pop, but not the kind of woman Azzie had thought she was about to meet.

Hooker heels. Pops' lady friend was wearing hooker heels! The ugly things must have cost a fortune, with thick platforms and stilted heels that were now wet with mud and salt stains.

Oh dear!

Pops had found himself a call girl. Azzie tried not to grin. If he had, she wasn't very smart. Who in their right mind would wear something so inappropriate, in winter, in Maine?

"Azure, come on in and meet Ashley Briggs."

Ashley Briggs? Her sort-of stepsister? The woman trying to steal the park?

Azzie stepped forward, her hand held out, a tremulous smile on her lips. Finally she was to meet the woman her father had raised while he ignored the "love" child he had created in Maine.

Ashley didn't shake Azzie's hand. The look on her face suggested she smelled something unpleasant, like fresh excrement and horse urine combined in a pile sitting in the hot humid sun.

Azzie's smile faltered.

"I had to stop by and deliver this news in person. I wanted to thank you for taking such good care of my partner Rockford when he came for a preliminary look at the property last week." Her smile looked reptilian. "He was so impressed he couldn't wait to get home and get our legal team working on the take-over. This will be our property before the new year."

Azzie's knees suddenly had a mind of their own and tried to collapse under her, but Azzie was made of sterner stuff. He may be named Rock, but she was made of tough New England granite. She was not going to become a weeping pool of goo at the feet of a woman Azzie could now see was her mortal enemy. Her childish dreams of having a sister were doomed. It was obvious the woman had no desire to be sisters, or even friends. So much for foolish dreams of someday having a sister to laugh with and confide in.

She had Pops and her cousin Thawe, who was more brother than cousin. Who needed anyone else?

Rockford! Azzie had tried to avoid thinking about that part of Ashley's shocker, but she couldn't erase it from her mind. Ashley had said her partner was Rockford. He couldn't be the same man who had rocked her world last weekend!

Rock. Rockford.

She had thought that maybe his mother, or his father, had been a big Rock Hudson fan, but he could have shortened it to Rock that night to hide his real identity. Now that she thought about it, he had never told her his last name and all the gifts were sent from the seller with a card signed "Rock". There couldn't be that many men in the New York area with such an absurdly pretentious alpha name.

In addition to finding out the man hid his real identity from her, Azzie had to find out the man was involved with the wretched woman sitting in front of Pop's desk in an obscenely short skirt and those ugly shoes.

Tears threatened to rise to the surface, but Azzie ruthlessly pushed them back down. She would not give her horrible, evil stepsister the satisfaction of seeing a single tear fall.

She was Azure Brown. Direct descendant of Humphrey Brown and his Medicine Woman wife. This was her land. Her home. Her park. Her business.

No scrawny assed bitch was going to waltz into Pop's office and take her heritage away. Nor would Azure allow her broken heart to show in front of the devil's spawn her sperm donor "father" had raised. Now she had all the more reason to be glad the man had stayed out of her life. If only Rock had had the same decency.

Azzie's hope for a future with a family she already loved might be shattered with the revelation of who Rock really was. He may have fooled her, but she wasn't stupid enough to remain a fool. She looked into the glare of Ashley's spiteful eyes, and refused to flinch.

No one was ever going to take the land away from her. No. One. Ever!

"We bought all of Brownville Junction's debts. You have two weeks to redeem that debt or we will own Brownville Junction, lock, stock, and barrel." Ashley chuckled heartily. "Damn, I knew it would feel good to say that, but I never realized it would be orgasmic."

Pop sat in his old desk chair and looked at the wretched woman, but he didn't say a word. Azzie was not fooled. Her grandfather's brain was going a mile a minute, and he didn't look worried. There was something he knew that she wasn't privy to. Yet.

She hoped!

"You look a little pale, dear. Didn't Rockford tell you who he is or why he was here?" Ashley flashed a sly smile. "That is so like him. Tricky devil likes to romance information out of women rather than treat them like adversaries. He thinks he's Casanova. He's a tomcat. He really likes to play around, but he always comes back to me. I'm the one woman he can't stay away from."

Azure would not dignify Ashley's aspersions to her character with a retort. If the woman wanted to imagine Rock had been her lover, then let *her* be tormented by it. Azzie may have day dreamed many a hot clinch between them, but since it had never happened, she still had her pride. She could hold her head up high and not wonder if the philanderer had given her some obscure STD that had no cure.

Ashley tottered to the door in her extremely high heels. "Save yourself time, dearie. Don't bother trying to grovel to my Daddy. Sorry, that would be Dean to you. He can't bail you out. He and *my* mother, the woman he chose to marry, are on an extended holiday. Even I can't reach them right now. And they love me." Azzie's fist itched to wipe the smirk off Ashley's face. "Rockford won't help you, either. He's as anxious as I am to complete this deal and have you out of our lives for good. After all, we have a wedding to plan."

The last thing Azure saw before the old wooden door closed was the sneer on Ashley's face.

Chapter 13

Ashley and Rockford. They were a despicable pair and deserved all the hell they would give each other.

The only sound in the office after the door slammed was the ticking of the old desk clock Pop kept on the bookshelf. The tick, tick, tick of the ancient mechanism echoed in Azure's ears.

"This Rockford was the fella staying with you during the blizzard, Azzie?" Pop's voice was unusually quiet.

Suddenly Azzie's heart started pumping again and the tears couldn't be fended off any longer. They flooded through Azzie's lashes as she turned to face Horace. "Oh, Pop, I am so sorry. I didn't know he was the creep trying to steal the Junction from you." Guilt covered her in a blanket of cold sweat. "I must have let my guard down and said too much." Her hand flew to her mouth. "I must have had papers, bills, and stuff in my bag or on my desk. He must have gone through them while I was busy with Meggie."

Horace Brown swiveled his old-fashioned, wooden office chair around and hefted himself up. The old leather squeaked as he moved. He wrapped his arms around Azzie to offer her the same comfort he gave the distraught child who cried every time her Mommy walked out the door. "Azzie, honey, you did nothing wrong. You have worked your butt off for this land since you were a toddler and we used you and Thawe in our promotional materials."

Horace's love and warmth enveloped Azzie. "But, Pop . . ."

"There is no 'but' here. You have an overblown conscious that makes you feel as if you are responsible for all the ills in the world," Horace sighed. "I have to admit I have used that to my own advantage this year. I wanted you home and involved with the park, so I used a little heart flutter to get you here."

"Pop, you didn't use me, I wanted to come home," Azzie gulped. "I took the job at the University because you had to scale back on the museum. You didn't need an overqualified docent—a high school student could handle the job just fine."

"There are always plenty of management jobs here, even without needing a full time curator." Horace hugged Azzie.

"I know, but I always knew the plan was for Thawe to be your successor while I managed the museum. I didn't want him worried about kicking me out of a job when he retired from the navy," Azzie sniffled.

"Keeping this park running is more work than one person can handle, and whoever is doing it needs someone they can trust as their second." Horace looked Azzie in the eye. "No one ever said the top job was going to be Thawe's. He likes being a JAG. He likes being in the navy."

"But . . ."

"There are no buts about it. Neither one of you have to be the top dog in this circus. This isn't an inherited bit of slavery. If neither one of you want to work in the park, we have two choices. We can either shut the park down, or allow someone else to run it." Horace released Azzie and returned to his seat. "I think now would be a good time to have the discussion we have all been putting off. Do you and Thawe want to keep the park running and who is going to be the head of the company? If not, do we just shut it down and auction off all the equipment or do we find someone else to run it?"

"Is there anyone else we could trust to run it and still keep the standards high?" Azzie felt cold inside. She couldn't believe Pop was actually thinking about letting someone else run the park.

"Girl, there are unscrupulous people in this world that will go to any lengths to get what they want. If they want something badly enough they will do anything to get it," Horace patted her hand resting on the edge of the desk.

"Even feed a precious child too much junk food in order to get them stranded in the middle of a blizzard." Azure was pleased to hear more backbone in her voice.

"Honey, I think that was more like good luck on his part. I don't see as how any man likes to have puke all over him. Especially in front of a pretty woman, and him without a change of clothes," Horace chuckled. "I would find that downright embarrassing. I'm sure he didn't look very suave or sophisticated in Thawe's ratty old sweats."

Azure snorted her response.

"You know, Azzie, people have been trying to take this land away from the Browns since old Humphrey Brown first claimed it as his own in 1578. Family legend says if you sit before a medicine fire and look deep into the flames Great-great-grandmother will send the *Mikum-wasus*, the forest spirits, to your aid."

"Pop, if the next thing you suggest is that I search for *Giwakwa* to come eat the evil Rock, you can forget it." Azure hung her head. "I don't hate him that much," she mumbled.

Her life was falling apart again and the ugly specter of *Giwakwa* was once again haunting her.

She shivered at the thought of the *Giwakwa*, the man-eating ice giant. Azure had been terrified by one on her ninth birthday.

She should never have run up the mountain, but her Mommy had disappeared. Again. And she had only been home for two days. When Rose had walked through the front door, Azzie was so excited thinking her Mommy would be there for her birthday.

On the day of her birthday, Azzie came home from school and went directly to her mother's room to show her the spelling test with the gold star on it. But Mommy wasn't there, so she went looking for her with the test clutched tightly in her hand.

She searched the entire house, including the spooky old attic and basement.

What could have happened to Mommy? She must have gone for a walk in the woods and get hurt or lost? That happened to people all the time. Azzie was worried and had to find her.

She searched the woods. Then she started going uphill. What if Mommy had climbed the mountain and gone too near the ice caves which Pop told her and Thawe to never go near? Her fear that her mother might be lost in the woods led Azure deeper into the forest in search of her mother. Deeper than Pop allowed her and Thawe to go.

It was almost dark, but Azzie wouldn't stop looking for her Mommy. A cave loomed ahead of her. One that she had never seen before, not even when she went hiking with Pop. Azzie headed for the cave, maybe Mommy was trapped in it. But instead of finding Mommy, *Giwakwa* lumbered out of his cave and tried to grab her. Azzie had been terrified.

She turned and ran. She fell and *Giwakwa* almost caught her. She had seen his razor sharp teeth. She had smelled his foul breathe when he opened his mouth to devour her! Felt the coldness of his breath as his head lowered to bite her. Azzie clawed at the earth until she was able to scramble to her feet and run again. She ran until her sides hurt and she couldn't suck in another breath. She collapsed under an old oak tree and made herself as small as she could. She hoped the monster wouldn't be able to find her in the dark.

A *Mikum-wasus* (a forest spirit) found her huddled under the ancient oak tree and led her home. Thawe laughed at her story, but Pop believed her.

Later that night, Thawe explained how both their parents only came home when they wanted money. *Thawe was two years older and smarter. He knew these things.*

Azure's mother had left for Paris without saying goodbye to her only child, but Azzie hadn't found that out until a few weeks later, after she had recovered from a bout of pneumonia which had hospitalized the little girl for several days. Once again it was Thawe who explained it all to her. He said Granny and Pop kept things about their parents secret so that she wouldn't be hurt. But Thawe knew Azzie was a big girl and should know so she would stop crying for her mother like a baby.

At the ripe old age of nine Azure's world imploded around her and she couldn't share the burden with anyone.

The summer after her high school graduation, Azure heard Rose in the kitchen badgering Granny for more money. Azzie was out on the back porch husking corn and listened as her mother berated Granny over not getting her child support back since the kid was now grown up and out of school. Granny's reply was to snort and to tell Rose that Azure was going to college and would still need support while in school. Rose could either grow up and get a job or learn to live within a budget.

Azure was horrified to hear anyone speak to Granny that way. The only thing that kept her on the porch and not in the house defending her beloved Grandmother was the secret. It was important that Granny didn't know that Azzie knew.

It was always about the money with her mother. If money was that important to the woman, then she should have it.

That was the moment Azzie decided she would work her way through college and not accept any money from her grandparents. Let Rose have it. Azure wasn't afraid of a little hard work.

However, her grandparents were so worried about her living in the city and going hungry because she was too proud to come to them rent money, they insisted on buying her a place to live. They eventually compromised on the land.

"No, granddaughter, I would never send you to the *Giwakwa*," Horace's voice pulled her back into the present, "that would be a job for your cousin Thawe. Besides, I don't believe Rockford Hollister betrayed you. A man who had used you in such a way would not be sending you gifts each day," Horace smiled.

"Maybe he's sending them out of guilt." Azzie wasn't surprised Horace knew about the gifts—he might be old and almost retired, but he always knew what was going on in his company and in his family.

"A man who could betray you in such a way would not feel guilt. Now be a good girl and track Thawe down. I want him home for the holidays."

"You know he always comes home for Christmas when the Navy can afford to let him go," Azzie replied as she walked out the door.

He may try to fool her into thinking she was in charge, but Pop was in boss mode. He wanted his legal eagle grandson just in case she couldn't save the park on her own.

Azzie knew many people would have been insulted by Pop wanting to have his male grandchild come in to save the day, but not Azzie. She was a realist and knew there were so many legal maneuvers Thawe could dream up that would never occur to her.

Although, Pop should know better than to underestimate a pissed off woman!

Thawe could handle the legal part, but she would handle any face-to-face confrontations.

Hollister & Briggs may have tried to destroy her world, but they merely put a dent in it.

After the scare with Pop's heart, she should have been soothing him, not him soothing her. The park had been his whole life. What kind of woman was she to think of a man, a stranger, a pirate out to steal her land, rather than what her grandfather must be feeling? The land was ingrained into his soul and that of the family, with the exception of her mother and uncle who would sell them all out to have money to support their party life styles. The park was especially important to Horace since his grandfather had created the Junction.

It was just as important to Azure and Thawe. It was the only real home either of them had ever known. When their parents preferred to live childless lifestyles, Pop had opened his arms and his heart to the unwanted children. Neither child was ever lonely. They had each other, they had their Granny and Pop, and they had the Maine woods.

Azure Brown would never give up one inch of land without using everything at her disposal to prevent it. She was prepared to fight the battle of her life, and this was one war she had no intention of losing.

If she had to, Azure would find the *Giwakwa* herself and set him on Rockford Hollister's slimy trail, but she couldn't send the ice monster after Ashley. She was afraid they would be instantly attracted. Like finding like. Soul mates! What if they bred?

Brownville Junction did not need any more ice monsters!

Chapter 14

"Are you sure it's the only way?" Azzie asked her grandfather over the dinner table three days before Christmas.

She was exhausted. Somehow the media had found out about Brownville Junction's financial woes. When people heard the end was near for the iconic park, they arrived in droves to ride the "Portland Express" and to view the legendary lights one last time. In a strange twist, many of the visitors had traveled from Florida to see the Junction's light display.

A petition movement had been started for the government to give the Junction a "bailout" in order to keep the family entertainment park going. Azzie was grateful for the thought, but feared a government takeover of the land. If they lost the park, it would break Pop's heart and financially devastate the area. But even more importantly, they had to keep the land in the family.

Just in case they couldn't, Thawe had begun researching how to turn the property over to the Penobscot's for use as Reservation land. Old Humphrey's wife was not the only Penobscot in the Brown family tree. Their names proudly hung on many branches, along with Narragansett, Iroquois, and even Lakota names. If the land could not remain as Brown private property, it was only right for it to become Native America land.

"It's not the only way, Azzie, but it is the best way to keep control in Brown hands." Thawe's plan had Pop's seal of approval. It didn't quite cover the entire amount, but with a small sacrifice on Azzie's part and a large sacrifice by Thawe, she would arrive in New York City on Christmas Eve with a cashier's check in hand. For the full amount.

She planned to surprise both that lousy rat Rockford and super bitch Ashley in their lair.

Merry Christmas!

===#==#===

Ashley groaned in contentment as Francois gave her the happy ending she wanted with her message. She contemplated the size of the tip she was going to give him. She finally decided she would have to give him more than she had originally planned. She would still need her tri-weekly appointments with his magic hands until she had Rockford's diamond firmly on her hand and the invitations were in the mail.

Perhaps she would keep him even after that. Just because Rockford had dated a lot of women, it didn't mean he was all that great in the sack. After all, his looks and his money were powerful aphrodisiacs. There was no reason to give up

Francois until she was sure Rockford was good in the stretch.

Besides that, she was still furious with the fool. He wouldn't answer her questions about his disappearance and he refused to talk about the take-over of that ridiculous train park. When he finally waltzed into the office after being gone for more than a week, he announced that they were no longer pursuing the take-over.

Like he had all say in the matter. They were partners—this time he would do what she wanted. Once they were rolling in the profits Rockford would understand her genius and that little bitch would be put in her place. Forever.

He would show her a new respect when he realized that Ashley Briggs always got what she wanted.

As of midnight the park and all the property owned by the Browns would be hers. Or rather, hers and Rockford's.

She should go shopping before going into the office. She needed some new lingerie for tonight. She expected to finally get Rockford into her bed and she needed to make sure everything was perfect.

Ummm. Perhaps she should also stop for a wax—make sure everything was super smooth for tonight.

===#==#===

Azzie's red wool coat stood out like a beacon when she stepped off the train in New York's Penn Station. She had never seen so many people dressed in black in all her life, not even at a funeral. Had New York City become Goth central and nobody let the rest of the country know, or were they still in mourning because the Sox broke the curse?

Even in Boston, a slower paced city, Azzie had always felt as if she was on a handcar trying to outrun a super express train. She liked life at a slower pace. The energy in the black clad people as they ran for exits and fought over cabs had added a frozen brake to the metaphoric handcar she still struggled with.

According to Mapquest, the offices of Hollister & Briggs were only twenty-five blocks away. Azzie looked at the queue for cabs—it was long and getting longer with each train that arrived. Since she didn't have any luggage to cart around with her, she set off at a brisk walk.

The city sidewalks made her even more appreciative of the softly lined paths of pine needles or snow she had left behind in Maine. Rockford's office was in the ugly building across the street from her. It had obviously been erected for height, not beauty. It lacked the curves and curlicues that Azzie appreciated in the older buildings she had passed.

Before she crossed the street, Azure Brown straightened her shoulders, lifted her head, and prepared herself to face the man who had stolen her heart when all he really wanted was her property. A granite backbone took her through the revolving doors, by the information desk, and what looked like a platoon of security people. She walked as if she knew where she was going. She did not stop to read the directory board or gawk at signs. She just walked over to the elevators and pushed a button.

No one challenged her.

The elevator deposited her at a floor with lush carpeting. Modern art hung on the richly toned walls. There wasn't a single picture of a train in sight. Or maybe there was, but she couldn't recognize it in the artwork.

A receptionist sat at a glass and chrome desk answering the phones.

"I'm here to see Rock," Azzie hoped her throaty voice sounded sexy and not as nervous as she felt.

The receptionist waved her through a set of glass doors with the name Hollister & Briggs emblazoned on them. Azzie felt out of place, but she refused to let it show in her posture.

The next office she entered had warmer colors and wooden furniture. Azzie's knees felt like they had ocean waves knocking against them trying to toss her into the deep ocean. It was difficult to maintain a balanced stroll when she felt like she was sinking.

"Hello, I'm a friend of Rock's." The blush that flooded Azure's cheeks was real as she spoke to the secretary stationed in an outer office. "I'm sorry. I meant to say Mr. Hollister. Could I just pop my head in and say hi?"

"Sorry, miss, all visitors must be announced," the woman's lips thinned. Her prim black suit made Azzie feel like Hester Prynne with all the scarlet she was wearing. The woman's haircut alone probably cost more than the total of everything Azzie had on, including her good luck opal necklace.

"Of course. I'm sorry, I wasn't thinking." Azure lowered her eyelashes in what she prayed was an innocent gesture. She still hoped to get in there and surprise the bastard. "I'm Azure . . ."

"You're Azure?" The woman ran an experienced eye up and down Azzie's plump figure. Apparently she was not used to women in red coats and Dr. Who scarves. She wished she knew in advance that New York City was a monochrome. Nobody warned Azure that wearing red would cause people to stare. She might as well wave a red cape in front of a bull. The bull's reaction would be mild compared to these New Yorkers.

Azzie was willing to bet this secretary was the one placing all the orders for the gifts and the daily flower inundation. Azzie was shocked when the gifts continued after Ashley's visit. She chalked it up to the hubris of the man—he probably thought a few flowers, a train set, pretty ornaments, and his devastating smile were enough to get him what he wanted. She would have brought them all with her to toss in his face, but she had decided to travel light. Instead she had them all boxed up to be mailed to him after the holidays. She didn't want to chance them getting lost in the holiday mail.

"It's a pleasure to meet you. You're not Rock's usual type. It's nice to see a woman who looks like a real woman and not a life size Barbie doll walk into this office for a change." The woman smiled warmly at Azzie.

A blush burned Azure's cheeks. Damn! She didn't want to face Rock with a face as red as her coat.

The secretary smirked. "Will you do me a favor and leave the door open? I want to see the expression on his face when you walk in."

Azzie's hand slipped off the doorknob the first time she tried to turn it. She wiped her sweaty hand on her wool coat and clasped the doorknob of Rock's office firmly. Her other hand, encased in a white rabbit fur muff she inherited from her great-grandma, caressed a bank check for an obscene amount of money. She had to gain control of her breathing before she entered his inner sanctum. It wouldn't do to go in screaming like a banshee, no matter how much personal pleasure it might give her.

She tried not to glance back at his secretary, but nerves wouldn't allow her to keep her unprotected back exposed. The woman had an amused look on her face. Well, her family's financial problems might be a joke to these people, but Azzie was not going to give the woman a scene to replay for her salivating friends. Granny had always told her to keep her dignity when the bullies at school liked to pick on her illegitimate status, and what worked then would stand her in good stead now.

Hand back on the doorknob, Azzie closed her eyes and said a silent prayer before she threw the door open. She stalked across the carpet until she was in front of the desk. Rock looked up, a smile warming his face, his eyes glowing. The man was a great actor—he actually looked like he was happy to see her, but Azzie knew better. The man could be a star on Broadway or in some Oscar winning movie with that much talent.

His come-hither-let-me-stick-my-tongue-down-your-throat look made her insides quiver, but Azzie's backbone was made of sterner stuff. She knew an act when she saw one. If she had ever meant anything to him, he would not have sent his girlfriend to foreclose on Brownville Junction. He would at least have been man enough to do it himself. Although the man Azzie had thought he was wouldn't have gone after the park at all.

"Azzie, what are you doing here? I was going to surprise you at your home tonight," Rock rose to his feet. "Let me just clear off my desk and we can grab some lunch while you tell me what brought you to New York. I was sure you'd want to be with your family on Christmas."

"I will be," she mumbled as she worked up the courage to do what she was here to do.

"We'll stop by Rockefeller Center so you see the tree before we leave for Maine. We can hit a few stores if you have any last minute shopping to do."

Azure's heart broke at the sight of his smile. She loved him. She had to accept that fact. She was hurt by his actions, but she still loved him.

How stupid was she?

She had to get out of his office and this damn city as quickly as she could.

Faster.

Before she did something stupid like jump his bones, or cry, or jump his bones and cry.

"Here's your blood money." She withdrew the check from her muff and slammed it on the desk in front of Mr. Rockford Hollister, the lousy rat.

A frown darkened his face. He almost looked confused, like he had no idea what was going on.

He was good!

Rock began to walk around his desk. Azure held her hand up in a stop command.

"Don't come near me." Azzie had to get out of the damn office before he could touch her. She wrapped her anger around her like a protective cape. She was afraid his touch would weaken her resolve, melt her into a ninny that would fall for his lame lines.

"Honey, I don't understand . . ."

"You have your money. I hope you choke on it. We keep the Junction, you are never to contact us or bother us again." She turned on her heel and ran out the door. Tears spilled over her lashes, dashing down her cheeks as she hit the elevator button. The doors opened immediately and she jumped in and slammed her finger on the L.

Chapter 15

Rock was momentarily stunned. When he finally realized something was drastically wrong, he ran, but he wasn't fast enough. The doors on the express elevator were already sealed by the time he had reached the elevator banks. He frantically pushed the down buttons.

Another elevator arrived and Ashley stepped off. "Rockford, I am so glad to see you. I need to talk to you about tonight."

He shoved her away as she tried to embrace him. *Has the whole world gone freaking nuts?* He wondered. They didn't have that kind of relationship. They never have and they never would.

The only woman he wanted in his arms was Azzie and if he didn't hurry and catch her it might never happen.

"Not now, Ash. I have something I have to take care of."

He jumped into the elevator. It took an eternity to reach the lobby. As soon as he stepped onto the ground floor he searched for the woman in the bright red coat with a sprig of holly attached to the hood, but he couldn't see her anywhere.

Two members of security joined him outside.

"Is there a problem, Mr. Hollister?"

"A woman in a red coat just left my office. Did anyone happen to notice which way she went when she left the building?"

"Yes, sir. I saw her hop into a taxi," the second guard answered.

"Did you get the number?" Rock heard the rasp in his voice. At that moment he didn't care if the other guys noticed it or not. He didn't have time for male pride.

"Sorry, sir. We weren't alerted to any problems concerning the woman," the same man answered. "Otherwise we would have detained her immediately."

Rock wanted to pummel the man for daring to think he could detain Azzie, but at the same time he was furious the man hadn't kept the woman he loved from fleeing.

The older guard looked Rock in the eye and said, "I'm sure we can get all the information we need off the security tapes."

"You can do that?" Rock asked.

"Yes, sir. After nine-eleven we installed the best surveillance equipment on the market. Since then we've updated it yearly. Within half an hour I'll have all the information about her driver and where he dropped her off that you will need. With any luck, wherever she went is also on our security link and we will be able to continue tracking her."

"Bring the information up to my office as soon as you have it," Rock snapped before he headed back into the building.

"Mr. Hollister, if you have her cell number I can easily get her GPS coordinates," the older guard said as he followed Rock to the elevator bank.

Self-recrimination tore through Rock as he once again castigated himself for not getting her number before they parted in Maine.

"I don't have her number."

"That's okay. We'll track her through the cab," the guard said as he turned toward the security desk.

If the man found Azzie, he was going to find a huge bonus in his Christmas stocking as a reward.

===#==#===

"Donna, get my pilot on the phone and tell him to be on standby," Rock said as he passed by his secretary's desk.

Donna Kilroy surreptitiously shoved the romance novel she was reading onto her lap. Rock knew her penchant for reading during the quieter moments in the office and he usually didn't mind, although it did make Ashley nuts.

"You already have him scheduled for seven this evening," Donna replied in her Bronx accent.

"And now I want him available all afternoon."

"It's gonna cost you," Donna replied. "You know these rent-a-fly-boys charge through the nose and especially around the holidays. Their standby fees are outrageous." She paused for a moment. "I'm just saying."

"I appreciate your concern; however, it is my money."

"Okey dokey, smokey. I'm right on it." Donna picked up the phone and started punching in numbers before Rock was through his private door.

===#==#===

Rockford Hollister, business man extraordinaire, was on the hunt. He needed information and he needed it now. He switched programs on his computer and started checking numbers. The more he searched, the harder his fingers punched in more information on the keyboard.

A knock on his door had him shout out an expletive before summoning the knocker.

The security guard from the lobby stood there with papers in his hand. "We were able to track her to Penn Station."

Rock felt the blood leave his face. She went to the train station. She had no intention of spending time in his city, or with him.

"Could you have one of your men hail me a cab?" Rock was already out of his chair and halfway across the office.

"Won't do you no good to go to the train station. She already got on a train. It left the station twenty minutes ago," the security guard's voice was grim. "May I ask what the woman has done? Perhaps the police or the FBI can get her."

"She gave me a check," Rock answered as he went back to his computer.

"She gave you a bad check?"

"No, she gave me a bank check." Rock waved the guard out the door as his attention went back to the computer screen.

Donna's voice drifted through the door. "She hurt his pride."

Rock grunted. He wished it was only his pride the damn woman had hurt. He had never felt heartbreak or betrayal like this before.

Azzie had broken his heart, but after going over the computer figures, he couldn't blame her. It looked like he had broken her heart first. He had a lot of stuff to fix before he could fix both of their hearts.

First he had to set his betrayer straight on the pertinent facts.

Chapter 16

"Rockford, I am so glad to see you." Ashley greeted Rock with a smile when he entered her office. A smile that never reached her eyes. "Since we are both going to my parents' dinner tonight, and I know you don't have a date, we should go together. I haven't been able to find a car and driver for the evening."

"I'm not going. I have other plans for the evening," Rock said. His voice and manner remained calm, not a twitch to betray his inner fury.

"Darling, of course you're going to be there tonight. It is one of the premiere events of the season. Everyone who is who anyone will be there."

"I don't really care about anyone who is going to be there. I have other things to do," Rock said. His temper began to show in his voice. He had to rein himself back in. "Right now you and I have a business matter to discuss."

"The business is doing just fine. There is nothing we have to attend to until after the New Year." Rock had never noticed the snake-like quality to her voice or the way her tongue darted out like a viper's. "Why don't you join me in Tahiti? I'm on an early flight tomorrow and I just happen to have an extra ticket booked."

"There are a few things about the Maine project we have to settle before the holidays." He was proud to hear only a slight edge in his voice.

"But there's nothing to settle. We put it on the back burner after your little jaunt to the back country, remember?" The sibilance in her words definitely sounded reptilian. "Now, about Tahiti..."

"Not the back burner." This time he allowed a harder edge into his voice to match the words he chose. "In case you don't remember, I killed the project in its entirety."

"That's not how I understood it." Ashley moved from behind her desk and sat on the delicate couch she kept in the sitting area of her office. "You seem to be really upset about something." She patted the cushion next to her. "Come sit next to me and tell your Ashley whatever it is that is bothering. After all, we can't have you to be in a bad mood before we attend my family's Christmas Eve Gala."

"I've already told you, I won't be attending this year." It felt as if his jaw was locking as he walked over to the conversational area. Rock looked at the flimsy chairs facing the spindly looking couch. He remembered when Ashley had purchased the suite of furniture. She had bragged that they were authentic French antiques. To him they were a waste of money. It might be fine for tea with the ladies, but no man wanted to perch on a bunch of spindly white sticks and they were not practical in a business atmosphere, unless you were running a beauty salon or a bordello.

"Don't be silly, darling. We always attend; we haven't missed a year since we were children." Her lips were smiling, but her eyes remained cold, calculating.

"That's true. We do always attend this event. It has become a habit. You go, because it is a command performance for your family and you are a snob and like to be seen at these things. I go to please my family. I always end up dragging along some poor woman who would much rather be spending the holiday with her own family, but comes along with me so that I can keep you at arm's length." He allowed his own cold smile to show.

He had always been careful of Ashley's feelings. He didn't like to hurt anyone, especially a woman he had considered a friend. But after what he had found out while he went through their accounts on the computer, the kid gloves were off. He no longer viewed Ashley as a friend with tender feelings, but rather as a treacherous deceiver with the added cache of being an embezzler.

She had not only stolen money from the partnership, but also from some of their most valued clients.

"Rockford, there is no need to joke with me. It is cruel to talk to me like that, even in jest. I understand your need to act the part of a playboy after the debacle of your marriage to Jenna, but now it is time for you to face the facts. *I* am the perfect woman for you. Everyone has been expecting us to marry for years. We are considered the perfect couple by our friends and business acquaintances."

Rock couldn't believe her! He cut her off before she could go any further.

"We have been friends— at least I had thought we were friends—and business partners. Nothing more. I am dissolving our partnership. The only formality left is for the police to come in and take you out in handcuffs." His voice was harsher than he had planned.

After a careful perusal of the accounts, Rockford had sent copies of everything to his personal attorney, who in turn called in an accounting firm that specialized in finding the irregularities. Holidays or no holidays, there was a team already in place going over the accounts with a trained eye and they had already uncovered enough to call the authorities in.

"I haven't done anything wrong!" Ashley gasped. "Everything I've done, I've done for us and our love."

How had this woman hidden her delusions from him for so long? Had she always been like this? How had he missed the signs?

A knock had both their heads turning to see Donna Kilroy standing in the doorway. "Mr. Hollister, the police are here."

"Thank you, Donna. Show them in, and then you can go home." Rock shoved his hands into his pockets and stepped further back from the conversation area.

Ashley stared at Rock as two uniformed police officers walked in.

"Really, darling, you didn't have to get me two strippers for Christmas," she tittered.

"I didn't. They are the real thing. You've stolen from the company and from our clients. That is unacceptable behavior, and illegal." Rock's jaw was as hard as his name.

"But it's Christmas," she gasped. "You can't do this to me. What will everyone think?"

"They can think whatever they want. I'm not going to be there to help fuel the speculation. I have my own fires to tend to."

Rockford left the office with the sound of the police officer reading Ashley her Miranda Rights.

They probably wouldn't be able to keep her for very long. He had been lucky he had contacted his lawyer, who in turn called his golf buddy, the state's Attorney General, and told him of the suspicious accounting practices. He also told him that Ashley was booked on a flight to leave the country the next morning. The A.G. agreed to have Ashley picked up as long as Rock turned in his passport too. He didn't want to take the chance that Rockford Hollister was also involved and was trying to throw their investigation off by tossing Ashley onto the sacrificial pyre.

===#==#===

Azzie was physically exhausted and hurting everywhere, especially her heart. After stepping into the Amtrak station in the Westwood suburb of Massachusetts, she glanced around and found Chris Carson chatting up a pretty girl near the newsstand.

She liked Chris—he was one of the good guys. Not wanting to interrupt him, she found a seat on the other side of the depot. Just because she was off men didn't mean she had to take it out on her cousin's best friend.

Furthermore, the poor guy was doing her a favor. He had picked her up in the middle of the night and flown her in his helicopter from her grandfather's home in Maine to this train station, just so she could shave hours off her trip into New York.

She sighed wearily and waited. Her total time on the train, both going and coming back, was close to ten hours. She shouldn't be so tired—the seats were a lot more comfortable than what she usually sat on in a train. She had often spent more time than that riding the rails.

Damn! She didn't make herself smile with that old expression. She had to snap out of this mood before she saw Pop. It would upset him to see her down.

Azzie glanced up to see Chris was still talking to the woman. It was okay. She really wasn't in that much of a hurry to get home. She had already talked to Pop on the phone, so he knew the check had been delivered, and great-aunt Peggy Ann was already there preparing Christmas Eve dinner. There was absolutely nothing at home that required her immediate attention so she had plenty of time to wait for Chris.

The poor guy had promised to be waiting in here when she returned so he could fly her home again, and like the honorable navy officer he had once been, he was here. Waiting. For her. The least she could do is give the guy enough time to set up a date with the woman.

Eventually the crowd emptied out of the building and Chris looked around. Azure knew the second his eyes had spied her sitting with her hands folded neatly on her lap. He smiled at the woman before he turned to walk over to Azzie.

"Everything go okay?" He asked.

The concern in his blue eyes made Azzie feel even lower.

"Smooth as butter." Azzie was proud her voice sounded almost normal.

"My offer still stands." Azzie looked up at Chris. "I'm willing to track the guy down and do a fly-by shooting. They're a lot more common than you would think."

The laughter that erupted from Azure might have had a bit manic, but it was a happier sound than the tears that had been building up inside of her all day.

"Come on, sweet cheeks, I'd better get you home before your old granddad calls out the National Guard to look for you." Chris smiled as he pulled Azzie to her feet. "I don't know if it's my skills as a pilot he doesn't trust, or my ability to remain a gentleman with you when we're alone together above the tree tops with nothing but the stars above us and the world at our feet."

"We all know you're a horn dog, but he's not worried about me. He figures Thawe is scary enough for you to keep your hands to yourself."

"Oh sweet, Azure, you wound me." Chris placed his arm around Azzie's shoulders as they walked towards the far parking lot.

"A bit melodramatic there," Azzie choked.

"Sorry, my last date made me sit through Shakespeare."

"Poor baby. A little culture won't hurt you."

"A little culture wouldn't hurt me, but watching a bunch of high school students trying to do Iambic Pentameter was too much pain for this swabbie. You know, there's a reason I didn't go through SEAL training."

"Because you don't like Shakespeare?"

"I like Shakespeare just fine, it's pain I can't handle." Chris flashed a grin and Azure wondered why she had never been attracted to this handsome guy. Instead she had to fall in love with a petty land grabber.

Chapter 17

Getting out of New York had been a nightmare. It had taken much longer to get the Ashley business squared away than he had planned. Then the midtown traffic moved at less than a crawl. Rock had been afraid he was going to have to call one of his poker buddies to get himself airlifted when his cabdriver shouted, "Hold on!" and drove onto the sidewalk in front of Saint Patrick's Cathedral. The bridesmaids attending the bride on the sidewalk jumped out of the way and the bride was hit directly with a plume of dirty slush before the cab dived back into a hole in the traffic.

After that, the rest of the drive was a haze— he barely remembered getting out of the cab. He did remember having the crazy urge to get down on his hands and knees and kiss the ground, but he was saved from that indignity by the appearance of his pilot.

"Hey, boss, I'm glad you got here early. I wanted to let you know that I've filed a different flight plan." Zack Kinkaid, owner and operator of

Kinkaid Air, held his hand out for Rock's luggage.

"I've got it," Rock said as he hoisted a duffle onto his shoulder. "Why did you change the flight plan?"

"Kilroy told me you wanted to get to this old amusement park as soon as you could today. I did a little research and we don't have to fly all the way into Portland. There's an upscale resort area not too far away from your final destination. I arranged to land there. They'll have a car waiting for you when we arrive and within an hour of our landing you'll be shagging your little honey."

Rock had to fight the urge to knock Zack's teeth down his throat. Yeah, that was mild for guy talk, but Zack had been referring to Azzie and guy talk was too crude to use on her.

"I also reserved a very nice suite for myself for tonight with the option of staying tomorrow night, if you want to hang around an extra day. I took the liberty of having it all charged to your card." Zack laughed as he slid into the pilot's seat.

Rock had followed Zack and found a folder on the co-pilot's seat. He picked it up so he could have the seat. "What's this?"

"The woman at the resort told me GPS and cell service were spotty in that area, so she sent detailed directions for you to get to the park with the minimum chance of getting lost in the mountains forever," Zack chuckled.

"I'm so glad you and Kilroy are getting so much enjoyment out of my failed love life," Rock growled.

"Hey, buddy, it's always fun to watch the mighty stumble once in a while."

"Why do I do business with you?"

"Because I'm the best damn pilot around and I treat you like one of the guys, and not like a paycheck." Rock had never noticed what a grinning fool Zack was.

Zack put on his headset and started his preflight checklist.

"Buckle up, Loverboy, we're cleared for takeoff."

===#==#===

The car was a small Fiat, barely big enough to fit Rock's long body. He was glad Azzie couldn't see him cramped into the car. Even with the seat back as far as it would go his knees were sticking out at odd angles to fit under the steering wheel, and working the clutch and the accelerator became an Olympic sport.

He had hoped that by surprising her he would come across as a romantic figure, but in this car all he lacked was a round red nose and a rubber chicken. What woman would prefer a circus clown to that Darcy guy that seemed to get all the women hot and bothered?

The directions Zack had printed out for him were good, but didn't adequately prepare him for the narrowness of the roads, the hairpin turns, or the glare of the sun bouncing off all the hardened snow in the fields.

It was late afternoon on Christmas Eve, and the Brownsville Junction parking lot was half full of cars and school buses. Rock was surprised to find the park still open. Was it worth staying open? Didn't the employees want to be home with their families?

The gates were wide open and there was no one working in the ticket booth. Anyone could walk in, so he did.

It was just as well. He could imagine Azzie hanging a wanted poster in the booth with a picture of Rockford Hollister with a big red X across the face. She had probably banned him from the park.

As soon as he was safely inside the park he immediately went to the museum building. It was Azzie's favorite building so he had hoped to find her there, but the door was locked and padlocked.

Next he made a circuit of all the food stands and rides, hoping she was overseeing things from one of those positions, but Rock didn't see a red coat anywhere, except on Santa, and Azzie wasn't with him either.

He was heading for the train station when he heard the engine coming down the tracks. He arrived at the platform and watched as a crowd of people disembarked. Rock mingled with the crowd and boarded the train on the last whistle blow.

The conductor made the rounds chatting up the other riders. He seemed to know most of them by name, and when one little rider called the man Grandpa, Rock suddenly understood that this was the employees' Christmas party. It was a grand gesture and should have surprised Rock, but somehow didn't.

When Mr. Carmichael reached his seat, he gave Rock a beady-eyed stare. "Almost didn't recognize you. What happened to your fancy leather jacket, boy? Did it get ruined or are you too good to wear something that had been puked on?"

Hope vanished and Rock wanted to groan. He had gone to great pains sending Kilroy out to get him a suitable parka, boots, hat, and mittens. He felt like a walking advertisement for L. L. Bean. It would take a miracle for this guy to let him off at the whistle stop near Azure's cabin. Rock still remembered how the conductor had tried to stop her from taking him home with her on his first visit to the park.

"I learned from my first visit that it was better to respect winter in Maine and dress appropriately." Rock hoped he had achieved a light-hearted tone. If he came across as a sarcastic bastard, this guy would turn the crowd against him.

"Hey, Mr. Carmichael, isn't it time we all started singing?" a voice called out from the front of the car.

"In just a minute, Jenny." The elderly gentleman handed Rock a booklet with a red cover and a Christmas scene on the cover. He suppressed a groan when he looked at the title— The Brownville Junction Christmas Songbook. "Open up to the first page and start singing."

"Me?" Rock was proud his voice didn't sound like a mouse's squeak.

"Ya, you."

"But . . ."

"You may be a horse's arse, but there are no buts allowed from you. Ta ti da da da da . . ."

"Sleigh bells ring . . ." Rock croaked out before other voices joined in.

Mr. Carmichael walked back to the front of the car, but every time Rock stopped singing he headed back again.

When they were nearing the Whistle Stop, Rock stood up and walked up to Mr. Carmichael. "I'd like to get off the train."

The singing had stopped and everyone in the car watched them.

A smile creased the old man's face for the first time since he had found Rock sitting in the back of the passenger car. "Of course. It will be our pleasure to drop you off there."

Mr. Carmichael pulled a phone out of his pocket and made a call.

"The engineer says no problem. We'll be there in five minutes. Please take a seat until the train comes to a complete stop." Then the conductor started singing Silent Night and everyone in the car joined in.

===#==#===

Rock felt the cold as soon as he climbed out of the train. The sky was overcast. It looked as if snow was about to fall, but the Christmas lights blazed merrily in the wake of the departing train.

Something didn't feel right, but Rock couldn't put a finger on what was disturbing him. Then it dawned on him. He had expected he'd have to bribe the conductor to let him off anywhere near Azure's home. That had been too easy.

===#==#===

Dusk was here, and so was the snow.

Rock retraced his steps to the Whistle Stop Depot. He was sure this was the stop where Azure had carried Meggie off the train while he trailed behind, stinking of puke.

He would try one more path before he gave up looking around here. He had spent three days shoveling the path from Azure's tiny home to the depot. He thought he had taken the right path the first time, but when he arrived, all he had found was an open space of flattened out snow with an inexplicably naked patch of earth in the middle. There was no house, no panel truck, and no chicken coop.

The next path he tried had a cabin with the sign "Sugar Shack" on it. Metal buckets hung on the outside walls, but there were no footprints in the crunchy snow. The only prints to be seen—besides his own—belonged to animals and birds.

Rock trudged down the third path until he ran into a bearded man with a large dog scampering at his side. "Something I can do for you, son?"

"I'm looking for Azure Brown. I can't find her cabin," Rock answered through frozen lips.

"Azzie's cottage is gone." The scruffy guy rubbed the dog's head. "Some douche bag was about to foreclose on the park so she sold her home to help defray the cost of saving the place."

Azure had sold her home? The place she had so proudly defended against any slur? His chest tightened. He had never felt so low in his life. Would Azzie forgive him for what Ashley had done in the name of his company? Would he ever be able to forgive himself? She had built the cottage herself. Her love for her home showed in every aspect of her life there.

"She's in Boston?" Rock croaked. How on earth was he going to find her there?

"No. I don't think we'll ever get her back to Boston after all she's been through this year." The guy took a stick from the dog's mouth and tossed it into the woods.

"You knew her in Boston?" Rock took a hard look at the man. Was he Azure's lover?

"She was one of my students. Then my T.A. It was my recommendation that got her the teaching position at K.U. I was rather hoping to bring her across the river to teach in Cambridge sometime in the next two years, but it doesn't look like she'll be leaving this park again." The man took the stick away from the dog and threw it down the path again. "It's a shame. She's not the best teacher I've ever seen, but she knows her subject better than anyone else in the world."

Rock had to swallow a couple of times before he could ask, "Do you know where she is now?"

"She's at the old man's house. You don't want to look for her there, though. The two of them are at each other's throats because she wants to get an apartment in town or take the Sugar

Shack and the old man wants her to live with him. Don't blame him—the Sugar Shack is almost as ancient as the trees around here and the apartments in town leave a lot to be desired. Nothing homey about either place."

"So I will find her at Horace Brown's?"

"Yeah, but she's not in a good mood. You might want to wait a few weeks to talk to her."

"Thanks." Rock turned to head back down the path.

"Hey, buddy!" Rock turned at the other man's shout. "You do know that was the last train of the season you came in on, right?"

"No."

"Conductor must not like the way you walk or something. It's not like them to strand someone out here. Especially with the park closed for the next three and a half months." The guy laughed. "I'll give you a flashlight, you won't be able to get back to the park before it's fully dark. If you stick to walking on the tracks you'll be okay. The bears are in their caves this time of year, so you don't have to worry about them. You do have to watch out for coyotes though. They can be quite bold."

"How are you getting out?"

"I'm fully stocked on supplies for the next month. I have a book to complete before the next semester begins." The guy handed Rock a flashlight from the pocket of his ski jacket. Rock watched as the man and dog turned back up the path and disappeared.

Rock, stunned at the thought of Azzie's home being gone, didn't realize how dire his own situation had become.

Chapter 18

Rockford hunched into the collar of his leather jacket as he hiked along the tracks, castigating himself for being a fool and not being honest with Azzie to begin with. If he had been honest with her from the beginning, she wouldn't have believed he had anything to do with the loan being called in, nor would she have sold the home she had built with her own hands.

Full darkness had dropped over the park by the time Rock arrived back at the train station. There wasn't a soul in sight. He walked toward the main gate and noticed the quiet that had settled over the area. Nothing living stirred within the park—even the reindeer were gone from their enclosure. He didn't know how the hell he'd get out if the gate was padlocked. He'd probably have to scale the fence. It would be difficult with his numb hands and frozen feet, but get out he would, even if he had to take off his clunky boots to climb the fence. He had to get to Horace Brown's house and find his Azzie. If they were to have a future together, she had to know Rock had nothing to do with the attempted foreclosure, and she had to know tonight.

He couldn't let this ugly episode mar her Christmas, even if she didn't forgive him. He wanted her to know none of it was her fault.

He'd give her the money to get her house back. He could take away that worry and let her enjoy her holiday.

He wanted his future and hers to be entwined. He had never wanted anything as much as that.

The closed gate was in sight. He jogged the rest of the way to it, but found it was as he had suspected—the gate was locked. It was a chain link fence; very high, but still climbable. He was halfway up when he heard laughter.

"If you wanted out, all you had to do was knock on the gatehouse, boy." The man was robust with a strong voice. "Hell, boy, you made it back here much sooner than I had expected. I was in the hopper and didn't see you return."

Rock hung where he was, halfway to the top. If the old man planned on calling the cops on him for trespassing, he could be locked up overnight and he'd never get to see Azzie. His gut told him time was crucial in appeasing her. He should finish the climb and get out of there before the locals could get their hands on him.

"Come on down, boy. It's wicked cold tonight and I wanna git home and have a nice cuppa hot chocolate. If you cling to the gate much longer your hands'll freeze onto the metal. You weren't one of those kids that went around sticking your tongue on light poles to see if'n it would stick, were ya?"

Rock let go of the chain link and jumped to the ground. Pain shot through his feet and up his legs. Damn. That hurt.

"Boy, you don't have the sense God gave you at birth. You don't jump on frozen limbs, somethin' might break off," the old man said as he patted Rock on the back and eyed the boots hanging around his neck. "You might want to wear those on your feet. At least that's how we wear 'em in Maine. On our feet, not as neck bling."

"I didn't think anyone would still be here," Rock gasped as he bent over to put the boots back on.

"Normally on Christmas Eve no one would be here, but we can't have a furriner roamin' around the park in the dead of winter. Someone had to be here to let you out or call out search and rescue if you didn't make it back." The old man pulled a large set of keys out of his pocket and walked to the gate. "I don't have ta sit at home and wait for Santa nor do I have to cook anything for tomorrow, so I was the best choice to wait for you."

"I appreciate it. I guess I wasn't thinking clearly when I came here today." Despair coated Rock's voice like sand on silk. It was too late to go knocking on Horace Brown's door. Azzie would be busy with her family and friends. Tonight was not the right time to confront her and tomorrow would be even worse. What had he been thinking?

"Boy, where you heading now?" The old man asked as Rock headed to his car.

"To the motel. I need a room."

"Unless you're planning on breaking in, you won't get a room there. The place is closed. No one working there tonight or any other time for the next three months."

"Then I'll go to the B and B down the road." Rock grimaced. A Bed and Breakfast was not his style. For some reason, women equated a B and B with commitment. They angled and schemed to get him to one for romantic weekends. The one time he had fallen for that old ploy the woman had expected a proposal. Everything had turned nasty when she didn't receive one.

"Won't do you much good to go there. Heddy closed the place yesterday. She always heads to Florida for the holidays. Her folks are snowbirds. She comes home in April with the crocuses." The old man chuckled.

"I guess I'll have to head back to the airport. Stay there for the night." Zack had saved the day by taking a suite at the resort. Rock would have to go back there and stay with his pilot. He had counted on Azure listening to him and forgiving him. It had never entered his mind that he wouldn't get to see her.

"You're giving up that easily, boy?"

"It's too late today. I should wait until after the holidays to find Azzie."

"I thought I heard you made a lot of money in NYC?"

"I have," Rock replied.

"Seems a miracle you made anything atall with your defeatist attitude," the old man said.

"Sorry I don't live up to your expectations, but I've never been in this predicament before." Rock shrugged.

"And what predicament would that be?"

"Being madly in love with a woman who doesn't want anything to do with me." Rock admitted.

"She told you that?"

"She didn't have to. Her eyes said it all." It was bad enough he felt like hell, but did the old man have to rub it in.

"Guess they grow the men different in New York. A New Englander would at least insist on hearing the words, even if they are accompanied by a teapot flying towards his head."

"A teapot?" The guy sounded like he was talking from experience.

"A long story, best saved for another day." The old guy grinned at him. "Come on, boy. It's Christmas. You come home with me. No one should be alone on Christmas, not even you."

"I don't want to impose," Rock didn't want to be alone, but he also didn't want to be with strangers. He wanted to be with Azzie and Meggie, but Meggie was in Hawaii with her mother, and Azzie would be with her family. He would be alone. Thinking of what might have been. And for the first time in years, he would be lonely.

It was what he deserved.

Azzie was everything he had been missing in life. She was warmth and sunshine, even in a frigid blizzard. Now she was lost to him.

"Too late to be thinking about that. You wanna follow me in your car or you wanna ride in my truck?" The old man looked at Rock's rental car—the only vehicle left in the parking lot—and shook his head. "We gotta go down some rough roads. You better ride with me. That bitty thing will never make it. I've got potholes that are bigger than that."

Rock climbed into the battered rust-bucket of a truck and wondered why the old man was driving anything that ancient. They didn't talk on the ride, which surprised Rock. He thought the old man want to rip into him some more.

Dark woods surrounded the road. There were no street lights, and no moonlight filtered through the canopy of trees, just snow drifting down through the naked branches.

"Tell me something, young fella, seems to me like you were going off with a head full of steam when you got here, and now yer acting like ya run outta fuel. Do you always give up so easily?"

"I told you, I remembered the look in her eyes before she ran out of my office. She hates me." Rock was stumped. He didn't know what to do. Maybe this guy had some secret wisdom to share.

"Didn't stop ya from comin' here," the old man said dryly.

"Since I arrived everyone has been steering me in the wrong direction. Protecting Azzie from me." Rock shook his head. "It suddenly occurred to be while I was hanging on that fence that perhaps everyone was right. At least for now. I know how much Christmas means to her and I don't want to ruin the holiday for her any more than I already have."

"Ya know, boy, a man sunk in self-pity is a sorrowful sight. Where's the man of gumption that walked all those cold miles down the tracks?"

"What do I do if she doesn't want me?" Rock wondered aloud.

"You never know until you talk to the girl."

Rock didn't know where they were. He was as lost on the outside as he was on the inside.

A glow appeared in the distance. The old man pulled into a crescent clearing and Rock realized the glow came from the windows of a large house.

"Be careful getting out. The blood is still frozen inside you. If you jump down you're gonna feel the impact."

"Okay. Thanks," Rock muttered. He hated to admit how grateful he was to the old man for the warning. He had forgotten. There hadn't been any heat in the truck and he couldn't remember the last time he had been so physically cold.

Emotionally, he was just as frozen, otherwise he'd be bawling like a baby over losing Azure.

He was afraid it would be forever.

The old man opened the house door and signaled Rock to go in first.

The aroma of a pie baking settled over his senses like a warm blanket. A stab of pain shot through his frozen heart as he remembered Azure's homebody-soul and all he had lost.

To the left was a parlor, warm and inviting. Flames danced in a large fieldstone fireplace, a huge pine tree twinkled in front of a bay window, and a woman arose from an overstuffed couch, a colorful blanket wrapped around her shoulders. "Pop, where have you been? Come in here and I'll pour you a cup of chocolate." Her voice warmed Rock's soul. When she turned, he saw her beautiful brown eyes were red-rimmed. His heart skipped a beat.

"You! What are you doing here?"

Rock was overjoyed to hear her growling voice. Her question gave him the opportunity to talk to her instead of being thrown out to the wolves. *Are there wolves in the north woods?* He wondered.

"I had to see you. I have to explain . . ."

"You don't have to explain anything to me. Business is business. You didn't make me any promises." Her choked voice shriveled his soul. He knew she was hurt by his betrayal, but he hadn't realized it went so deep. If he had realized it was too late, he never would have left New York.

He couldn't expect her forgiveness, but he was here. Azure deserved an apology and an explanation.

"Azzie, let the man explain. If we don't like his explanations we can always hide his body in the woods. The only people who know he's here are Carmichael, Bobby, and that Professor guy. I'm sure we can find a way to make them forget," the old man said.

In dawning horror, Rock realized the old man had to be Horace Brown, Azzie's grandfather. He quickly tried to remember every word they had exchanged. He hoped he hadn't insulted the old man. He needed him as an ally if he had any hope of Azure hearing him out.

"Take him out to the woods now, Pop. I don't want him here. He's done enough damage to our family. I'm not going to allow him to ruin our Christmas any more than he already has."

Rock's stomach plummeted along with his hopes. This wasn't the warm woman who had nursed a sick child and welcomed a strange man into her home. She had turned into an avenging goddess who turned her back on him.

"Azure, we have a guest. Your grandmother would be mortified if she could see you making him feel unwelcome. Not to mention how cold he is since he had to walk from the Whistle Stop back to the depot alone. The man is frozen clear through."

Azzie's shoulders sank and she turned to stare at him as her grandfather spoke. The next thing he knew, she was beside him. She took him by his cold hand and dragged him over to the fireplace. She helped him shed his new parka and took the afghan off her own shoulders to wrap it around his. The warmth from her body on the blanket encompassed him in a cocoon that chipped away at the exterior cold. Her fragrance invaded his soul and warmed him from the inside out. The scent of chocolate, vanilla, and cinnamon clung to her. Warm and womanly.

She smelled like home.

She smelled like Azzie.

He wanted to bury his face in the curve of her neck and inhale all the sweetness and comfort she had to offer, but he knew they had to talk first. He had to tell her the truth about himself, but the old man still stood in the doorway watching. It wouldn't do to blubber in front of him.

Rock knew he had to grovel, but he had hoped the initial pleas would be made only to Azzie, not in front of her grandfather too, even though he had a right to know about the business end of things.

He grabbed her hand, like a drowning man, and sat on the stone ledge in front of the raised fireplace. "Azzie, I had no idea Ashley had bought up all of the Junction's debts. If I had known, I would have stopped her." He gazed deep into her brown eyes. He wanted to soothe the furrow between her brows with kisses.

"How could you not know when she was spending so much company money?" Azure huffed. "That check I gave you had a ton of zeroes on it."

"I'm the guy who puts together and sells the deals, Ashley handles, handled, the money end of things." She cast him a doubting look. "Really. Ashley has a crappy personality. Most of the people we deal with can't stand her. So we evolved into a system where I handle all the jobs that required people skills and Ashley is the number cruncher. She keeps track of the accounts and scouts out the best financing route."

Azure snorted.

"Okay. I admit I was lax in keeping track of what Ash was doing with the books. I've known her since we were kids, and I trusted her." Rock did not like the doubt that still lingered in Azzie's eyes. How could he convince her of the truth? "She was my business partner. I thought she was trust worthy.

"Last spring I had offered to sell Ashley my half of the company. I was bored and wanted out. That's when she first broached the subject of getting this land and building a resort. It was a new challenge and it appealed to me. I was bored with the business and with New York. I thought I wanted to expand my horizon. Moving into high end resorts was tailor made to relieve my boredom."

Azzie grunted and tried to take her hands back.

"I wanted to jump right in, but your grandfather refused to hear our offers. It got to the point where he was sending our letters back unopened, with 'not interested' written in big red letters across the envelope."

"That's my Pop," Azure's beautiful brown eyes glowed with pride as she looked at the old man sitting in a nearby wing backed chair listening to every word. Rock hoped the old guy's hearing was bad. His male pride had already taken a beating and he hated the idea of an audience while he pleaded his case.

"As you know, a couple of weeks ago Jenna dropped Meggie off with me so she could celebrate her second divorce with a cruise. I had been planning to come here myself to check out the property. On paper everything sounded wonderful, but I really needed to see it for myself. Meggie's visit gave me the chance I was looking for. A man coming here alone would have looked like a child molester on the prowl. Meggie was the perfect cover."

"You let her eat herself sick in order to go home with me?" This time she managed to get a hand free.

"Sweetheart, I didn't know who you were when you walked away with my daughter, but you were kind to a sick child. Since you knew the place so well, I thought you were an employee. I never imagined I had hit the jackpot and had the owner's granddaughter to pump for information." He regained custody of her hand in time to stop the slap he could see in her eyes. "But I kept forgetting to pump you for information because all I wanted to do was jump your sweet ..."

Ahem came from across the room. Apparently the old man intended to hear every last word. But not those intimate words.

"I didn't know Ashley had a private agenda. I had never heard of you. I've known her most of her life and I didn't know you were sisters. Dean never mentioned he had other children."

"We're not related," Azzie said emphatically. She was really cute when she glared like that. He wanted to kiss the scowl off her face.

Ahem sounded again.

"After you rushed out I tried to go after you, but you were already gone." He hoped her kind heart could hear the pain in his voice. "You had performed a miracle. You caught a cab as soon as you had exited the building. Unheard of in New York City. Especially on Christmas Eve. When I arrived back upstairs I went through our accounts for the first time in a long time. Then I went to Ashley's office and we had a major blow-out about you and the Junction. It turns out she only wanted the land so you wouldn't have it. It completely blew me away. I've known Ashley since we were kids and I never knew she had so much hate in her heart for her long lost sister." Rock watched her chin lift higher and held onto her hand tightly. He really didn't want her to give him a shiner, at least not until he was sure she would make him feel better with a kiss.

"I told you, that woman is no relation of mine. Her mother already had her when she married my biological father. The man is a cad. He had spent the month of July hiking these mountains and had a 'summer fling' with my mother, who was too young and stupid to know better. She tried calling him and he never returned her calls. One day, when she was six months pregnant, she stole Granny's car and drove all the way to New York City. She found my father, but he had already married Ashley's mother. Apparently, he had been engaged to the former debutante divorcee all summer."

"He supported you and had visitations, didn't he?" Rock knew the man. He gave to charity, he was a good stepfather to Ashley, and he had been a mentor to Rock.

"No. Mom was devastated and never went after him for support. Pop and Granny were willing to take care of me," she answered proudly. "We didn't need him."

"So it wasn't his fault. His not supporting you, I mean."

"If he had been a decent man, he would have contacted my mother. He knew she was pregnant and didn't bother to follow up. He didn't know if I was alive or dead until I was seventeen and went to the city on a class trip. I snuck away from the group and went to see him. He was shocked to meet me. We talked for a while. He asked if I expected him to pay for my college and I told him, quite graphically, what he could do with his money. We Browns are not the forgiving kind."

Rock had to bite the inside of his cheek. She was still the sweet woman he had met two weeks before, but she had an edge and an attitude he hadn't suspected. The woman had depths and facets he wanted to explore for years to come. He hoped she would forgive him and give him the chance to do so.

"My senior year the man had the nerve to show up out of the blue. He came to my high school graduation and I was so upset I almost didn't give my speech."

"Now, Azzie, it is time to stop bashing that poor man. At least he showed up, which is more than Rose did," Horace chimed in.

"Pop, it is well known that I have two neglectful parents. Thank you for the reminder. I almost forgot," she said tartly.

Rock kissed her nose. She had the cutest little nose. He had to keep her off balance. He didn't want Azzie to remember all his sins before he was finished with his groveling. While he was in here holding her hand he had a chance to plead his case. If she threw him out he'd have a case of hypothermia to freeze his broken heart.

Chapter 19

"Hey, Az, I'm home. Dinner ready?" A deep baritone voice shouted from the foyer.

Azzie jumped to her feet and ran for the door.

Rock watched in jealous frustration as she flung herself into the guy's arms and a heavy duffel clunked on the floor as he returned her embrace.

"That better not be laundry for me to do." Azzie laughed up into the sailor's face.

Was sailor boy her lover?

"Only if you've lost our heritage." Rock wanted to bash the guy's pearly white teeth down his throat.

"No, only part of it." Rock felt a little better when Azzie pulled away from the guy. "I'm really sorry about your retirement fund."

"I'm not worried about it, but I'm afraid the news has spread to the parental units. I heard from mine. They should be here in time for dinner."

"Tonight?" Azzie squeaked.

"Tonight," the sailor confirmed. "They're worried about their allowances."

"Oh crumble cakes!" Rock knew that was strong language coming from Azzie, he had never heard a bad word come out of her mouth before. "I suppose Rose is going to expect tofurkey tomorrow."

"She's not vegan anymore. I guess her new guy is a caveman because she eats only paleo now," the young guy chuckled.

"The caveman diet?" Azure's squeak was kind of cute. "I have nuts and berries, but I'm not going to go club a bear to feed her!"

"She eats what we have, or she'll eat nothing at all," Horace said as he got up from his comfortable seat by the fireplace. "If your mother wants something different from what we're having, she can cook her own food."

"Pop . . ."

"Azzie, girl I love you, but you have too much of your grandmother in you. Both of you, always fussing and fretting over everyone else." The old man shook his head. "You cater to the whims of those children of mine and they'll always stay children. They're both fools and will never make it alone in the world. Once I'm gone, their care in gonna fall onto the two of you. If there is any hope for them, you have to cut the apron strings and let them either drift away or learn how to swim."

"But . . ."

"Pop's right, cuz. I want to have children someday, but I want to raise them from babies, not a couple of fifty-somethings."

"Thawe, do you have an announcement to make?" Azzie grinned at the guy.

The guy was her cousin, not her lover, and she was joking with him. Rock's heart lightened by a ton.

"No, but I've done a lot of thinking and re-evaluating my situation. Since you called me about this mess with the park I have been forced to think more about the future. I realized that I want kids and I want them to have what we had. A good loving home where they can run around barefoot and play in the woods. As much as women love men in uniform, it's time for me to ditch the uniform and come home."

"I may have messed up with your parents, but your grandmother and I definitely got something right with you two." Horace embraced the pair as if they were the size of Meghan. Rock couldn't remember the last time his father or mother had hugged him like that. This was the kind of family he wanted Meggie to grow up in.

No, that wasn't right. This wasn't the kind of family he wanted Meggie to grow up in—this *was* the family he wanted her to be a part of.

Rock was still lost in his own thoughts when Horace turned and spoke to him. "You're good, boy. I can see you are used to getting your way with women. I don't know if your playboy charm will work on my little Azzie. She hasn't been her sweet self since that b-woman was here. Azzie turned my ears blue and scared the living daylights out of me when she described all the things she planned to do to you if she ever saw you again. Yet you're still here, and so far unharmed. I can't wait to hear you talk your way out of this trouble."

"Don't go encouraging him, Pop. *I* don't want to listen to him. There isn't anything he can say that will exonerate him." Azzie cast a pleading look at Rock. "Please leave."

That look was all the encouragement he needed. She was softening. She really wanted him to know what the magic words were that would make everything okay.

"I love you, Azzie."

The only sound to be heard was the popping of the fire as it consumed sap from the log.

Azzie stared at him.

"Sorry, son, I think you jumped the gun and blurted out that revelation a bit too soon. Try again." Horace Brown was enjoying his discomfort and Rock couldn't blame him after all Hollister and Briggs had put him through.

"Azzie, please come back over here and sit down. I want to explain everything to you." He hated the pleading note in his voice, especially in front of the other two men. However, he couldn't ask them to leave—this was their house, their territory, and he had harmed them, too. They had a right to hear him grovel.

"Go on, Azzie, sit by the man. If he doesn't hurry up and finish his story it'll be Easter and we'll be having egg bread instead of eggnog."

"Pop, don't let him off the hook so easily. He's not done with his excuses." Azzie's hands were on her hips. She looked ready to scream.

"Who made the eggnog?" The sailor asked.

"You don't think I'd let Azzie make it, do you?" Horace answered. "She's a skinflint with the nog."

"Then I say bring on the nog and let the scalawag entertain us all with his story while we imbibe."

"Thawe, Pop, why don't you two go get blasted out in the kitchen and allow us to continue with a grown up conversation?"

"Good idea, cuz, for you, not for us. We want to hear him out," Thawe said. "Give us three minutes in the kitchen before you begin."

Rock watched Horace and Thawe leave the room with relief. Begging for forgiveness didn't come easy and an audience only made it harder.

"Rock, those two will be back any moment. Knowing them they will leave the eggnog behind and just bring in the brandy bottle. No excuses, no apologies. Why are you here?"

"I already told you. I love you."

The stunned look on her face emptied his brain, which he was beginning to doubt he had, anyway. He had never told a woman he loved her, not even his ex-wife, and by the look on Azzie's face she wasn't ready to hear it.

"Too soon, huh?"

"Ya think?" she responded. Her smile looked a little warmer. It still had frost lining the edges, but it was warmer.

"Okay, rich boy, what are you doing here?" Thawe walked back into the room and sat in one of the winged chairs flanking the fireplace. "You're not getting our land. Even if you get Azzie, you won't be getting the land."

"I wanted to give you back the money you paid to Hollister & Briggs." Rock looked Thawe in the eye. "I have seen the financials. No one in your family has that kind of liquid cash. I wanted to make sure you had it in time for Christmas."

"Afraid Marley and the ghosts of Christmas past and future would visit you tonight?"

Rock wondered if Thawe meant that to be funny or insulting.

"So you brought the check back?" Horace now occupied the opposite chair—the genial old man gone, his hard eyes measuring Rock for the truth.

"No, I was going to, but then I realized my former partner would still be able to come after you for the money. I planned on giving you my personal check with extra for lost interest and penalties."

"You have that kind of liquid cash?" Thawe asked.

"I've made some good investments." Rock was proud of making his own fortune.

"So you think you can gain the property by placing a lien claim on it." Thawe's tone reminded Rock there was a lawyer in the room. A very well trained JAG lawyer. How could he have forgotten that from the investigator's report? Jealousy really did cloud the mind.

"I don't want to own the property. When Meggie and I stayed with Azure I found out Brownville Junction is not just a business, but as you said when you walked in, it's the family's legacy. After we got back to New York Meghan couldn't stop talking about the fun she had here. So I took her to several theme parks in Florida. She said they weren't as good as Azzie's trains. She wanted to come back home, meaning here."

"So your daughter has formed an attachment to my cousin. What is it you want? You want to buy my cousin for your daughter?"

"That's just it. She didn't just want Azzie, she wanted the whole park atmosphere. Even in the snow and cold, she really loved her experience here. This park is small town America and home with a capital H." His enthusiasm grew with each word. "Turn it into Glad Town. Hold town fairs all summer long. Sell slices of homemade apple pie and wedges of seven layer cakes, like at the fair in Pollyanna. Huge slices of watermelon and fishing games. Have brass bands doing performances on your Main Street. The train can stop in an old western town that features a saloon and dance hall girls."

"This is a family park, dance hall girls wouldn't be appropriate." Was that a little smile trying to push its way onto Azzie's stern face?

"They would be dancers, nothing that children couldn't see." Rock smiled at Azure. "They wouldn't be wearing anything too revealing. They'd be doing the can-can, not twerking."

"So you don't want Azure, you want to buy the park for yourself?" Thawe asked. "Without your partner."

"Don't be confused by my enthusiasm for the park. I want Azure. I'm not looking to buy the park, or anything else. I want Azzie and I want to help her bring this park to what it once was and what it can be again." Rock looked deep into Azzie's eyes. "I want our children to have this park as part of their heritage. I want them to learn how to swirl the cotton candy, work on the engines, listen to stories about old Humphrey, and ride on Big Hank every Patriot's Day."

Rock watched tears roll down the curve of Azure's beautiful cheeks before she turned and bolted out of the room. She apparently had a bad habit of running off whenever he said something she didn't like, but he was stunned. He didn't know what it was that he had said that had bothered her.

Was it because he mentioned their kids? He didn't know what kind of reaction to expect when he popped the question and that wasn't how he had planned to propose, but he had never imagined she would run off and leave him alone in a room with her male relations.

He jumped to his feet to follow her.

"Leave her be, boy," Horace commanded.

"I-I don't understand. What did I say that was so awful that she couldn't stay here and talk to me?"

"Old Hank," Thawe said. "She always had a strange attachment to that hunk of metal."

"Her heart is broken and the wound is too fresh for her," Horace added. "She loved that old engine."

A chill ran down Rock's spine. He was afraid to ask, but he had to know.

"The Japanese?" His voice sounded as frozen as his heart.

"How did you know about their offer?" Rock didn't blame Thawe for the suspicion that hardened his voice. "Was it the Japanese offer that scared you and your partner into trying to force us out before you could dig too deep into the terms of ownership of the park? You must have been really worried we'd sell Old Hank to save the park from you. Hope it makes you feel good to know that we did sell the old boy to get rid of you and your claims."

The mental blow was so strong Rock staggered backwards.

"I never wanted to do anything that would cause Azzie pain. Before I met her, I assumed she would be happy to lose the albatross that kept her from her career in Boston." Rock shook his head. "I can't believe I was that stupid. It quickly became clear that Azzie loves it here and didn't look forward to returning to the city. Once I returned to New York, I realized I loved it here too."

"Shut it, Thawe." At Horace's words, Rock saw Thawe snap his mouth shut. "I believe the boy. He doesn't need any more guilt piled on him at the moment."

"He hasn't asked yet what happened to Azzie's pride and joy," Thawe pointed out.

"Are you talking about Azzie's house?" At Thawe's head nod Rock continued, "There was a guy in the woods. He told me she sold her little house to help pay off the park's debts." His voice was dull with shame.

"Yeah, and I closed out my retirement fund." Thawe drummed his point home with his fingers doing a drum roll on the arm of his chair.

"I have the money. We can rebuild your retirement fund. I will pay your penalties and add interest to it. We can get Azzie's house back too. I swear I'll get Old Hank back even if it breaks me." Rock reached into his pocket for his cell phone. "Give me the contact number for the Japanese consortium and I'll make the arrangements tonight."

"We can't get Old Hank back from the Japanese. They don't have him," Horace said. "Even though they offered the best money, Azzie refused to sell to them."

Chapter 20

Rock sank to the fireplace ledge in relief.

"Azzie brokered a deal no one else had ever considered," Thawe said. "She contacted a couple of other amusement parks with a train theme around the country and worked a deal so that each park would have Old Hank for a year at a time. Every five years he comes back to us."

Relief flowed into Rock, but before it could take hold a new worry niggled it's way in. "What happens if one of the other parks goes under or is taken over by another company? That other company could tie Old Hank up in litigation for years."

Rock was insulted when the other two men laughed at his concerns.

"Azzie may look soft and sweet, but her brain is always miles ahead of everyone else." Horace's smile was filled with pride. "Do yourself a favor and never play chess with her. We always knew she was good at getting her way, but it turns out she is a powerhouse at negotiation."

Good to know, but that still didn't lessen Rock's fears.

"Azzie thought about those contingencies and added a clause to the deal. If a park and/or company is sold, goes under, or is taken over, Old Hank is merely there as a piece of rental equipment. That park loses all rights and claims to Old Hank and their year reverts to Brownville Junction," Thawe said. "I'm trying to convince her to go back and get a law degree. We'd make an unbeatable team in court."

If he had to, Rock would follow Azure anywhere she needed to be. If she wanted to return to Boston for law school, then Boston it was, but he had hoped they could make a life together here on her family land, or he could buy land close by for them. Maine had stolen his heart almost as much as Azzie had.

"Thawe, I've already told you, any further education I get will be in my own field." Azure walked back into the room with a nervous smile and red-rimmed eyes. "The ham is on the table, waiting for you to cut it, Pop. Thawe, go with him and start learning. Someday you're going to have a wife making ham for you and you had better know how to carve it."

"How'd you do all that cooking and go to New York?" Thawe asked.

"Aunt Peggy is napping upstairs. She came and took over the cooking for me while I made the trip to New York," Azzie said.

"Yeah, keep your voice down, Thawe, we don't need my sister sticking her two cents in right now," Horace said as he stood up to lead the way out of the room. "This is entertaining enough without that old harridan sticking her nose into it."

Once they were alone together, Rock felt as nervous as a mink near a fashion runway. "I have so much to say to you, but I'm afraid they'll be back in here before I can say it all."

"If you've warmed up enough, we could take a walk outside. The snow has stopped and the moon is out. We can go watch it sparkle over the wooded paths." Her smile melted the leftover frost from his soul. Hope flooded his heart.

They scooted out to the coat rack in the vestibule and shrugged into their coats before slipping out the door. Azzie grabbed Rock's hand and dragged him down a wooded path. She stopped abruptly and pulled his head towards her. Azure's beautiful lips closed on Rock's. He was stunned for a moment before he pulled her into a tight embrace and took control of the kiss.

Several minutes later, Azzie stepped away.

"What was that for?" he asked.

She pointed to the trees above their heads. "Thar be mistletoe up there."

"Perhaps we should do more to appease the Gods of the mistletoe." Rock pulled her into his arms.

"Didn't you have something to say to me?"

So many words flooded his mind. There was so much to say to this beautiful woman, but only three words would come out. "I need you."

"You need me?"

"That didn't come out right," Rock said.

"Oh, you meant you want my park?"

"No, babe, it's you I need. I never realized until I met you that I wasn't a whole person. I went through the motions. I played the games. But I wasn't complete." He ran his hand through his hair, knocking his stocking cap off in the process. "Hell, before that weekend I had never spent more than three hours with Meggie, and none of that time had ever been alone. In fact, I spent more time with my daughter that weekend than I did in her entire life up to that point."

He caressed her cheek with his fingertips.

"I fell in love with you when you whipped off your pink scarf and started wiping Meggie's vomit off my crotch."

"You mean you are looking for a mother for Meggie."

"Meghan has a mother, I want you for me."

"Are you sure it's me you love, and not my land and amusement park?" He hated to hear the insecurity in the voice of a woman who had never shown any lack of self-confidence before.

"I have to admit, I am a bit devastated because I won't see the inside of your sleeping loft tonight. I was hoping to spend the next week ensconced in your little pink and white world."

"Someone else now owns the house, but if you really want to be ensconced there . . ."

"Only with you, Azzie. I only want to be ensconced with you." It had been too long since their last kiss, so he lowered his head and found her warm lips waiting.

The woman knew how to kiss and he intended to kiss her for a long, long time.

A dog barked in the distance and Azure pulled away. "Thawe will be here in a few minutes."

"I guess he is worried about you being out here alone with me," Rock whispered in her ear. "Is he still afraid I am trying to trick you into giving me the land? Let me assure you, Sweetheart, I am a very rich man. If all I want is a pretty piece, I can buy it anywhere in the world."

"Half an hour ago you were enthusiastic about bringing Brownville Junction back to its former glory," she murmured.

"That's because I love you and I want to do everything I can to make you happy."

"Then I guess now is the right time to break it to you. Even if we hadn't redeemed the debts, all you would have owned is the equipment, not the land." Her breath misted his ear.

At first her words didn't mean anything to him. "What do you mean?"

"Great, great uncle Charles was a lawyer; he is my great, great grandfather's brother. As is the tradition in the Brown family, the eldest brother cares for the land, while the second brother takes care of the trust." She pulled away to look at his face. "When Harold wanted to open the amusement park, many of the family members included in the trust were worried about losing land if the venture failed, so Uncle Charles set the park up with a lease. Brownville junction pays the trust one dollar a year."

"In other words, Hollister & Briggs would have to pay the trust one dollar a year in order to use the land," Rock said.

"Nope." Azzie's smile reminded him of a shark. "There is a contingency in the lease."

A chill went down Rock's spine that had nothing to do with the cold breeze that passed through the trees. This was a side of her he had never seen before. "A contingency?"

"If the park were ever to pass out of Brown hands, the new owners would be responsible for the removal of all traces of the park, buildings and equipment, even the parking lot and train tracks." There was a satisfied gleam in Azure's eyes.

Rockford laughed at the idea that everything he and Ashley had done would not have gained them the land, but would in fact have ended up costing them a great deal for nothing.

Azzie wasn't finished yet. "If we hadn't come up with the money in time, there would have been a process server looking for you tomorrow to give you the notice to vacate the property. In fact we decided to have you served with a nuisance suit. We're sick and tired of people trying to steal our land. We're very private people. We don't like to draw attention to ourselves or our land, but it is time to put an end to people thinking they can take it away from us."

"Please excuse me, but I'm about to sound like a total idiot. You're hot when you declare war." Rock wanted to kiss Azzie so bad.

"You are an idiot," she said with a smile.

"Did you call off your process server?

"She's in New York. I will call her when we get back to the house and tell her she can tear up the document meant for you. However, I still intend to have her drop it in Ashley's hand. I want that bitch to know that even if we hadn't come up with the money to save the park, she never would never have gotten her hands on our land!"

Although some might have seen Azure's need to rub her opponent's face in it as revenge, Rockford Hollister saw it as spunk. He liked spunk in his woman.

"I pulled a few strings and had her arrested before I left. She may not be out of jail by the time your woman finds her." Rock grinned.

"Lucy is a Brown cousin and very determined. She'll find her. You had Ashley arrested?" Azzie lifted her eyebrow as she asked the question. He couldn't resist. He had to kiss that eyebrow. Then her nose needed attention. Her rosy cheek beckoned when she pulled away. "Why did you have her arrested?"

"After you disappeared I did some digging into the books and I found out she was playing fast and loose with the company money. I knew she was flying out to Tahiti tomorrow and I wanted her stopped before she could get out of the country," he explained before going back to that poor neglected cheek.

"Wasn't there any way to stop her other than having her arrested on Christmas Eve?"

"Sure, I could probably have paid some poor schmuck to have sex with her, but I'm not really sure if the guy would have been able to keep it up long enough to keep her in New York." He looked her straight in the eyes and pressed his groin against her so that she wouldn't have any doubt about his feelings. "It isn't a job I would do."

Her blush was adorable.

"Is there anything else you have to know right now? I want you to be satisfied." He wanted to satisfy her in every way possible, but he didn't want to say too much now and scare her off. He was in awe of the strength of his feelings for her.

"I'd like to see Meggie again," she whispered.

His heart swelled.

"After the holidays I will have full custody of Meggie."

"How on earth did you manage that?" Azzie asked.

"I told Jenna I wanted my daughter to live with me, and she agreed. It seems a young child can do a lot to hinder husband hunting."

"I thought you said you weren't looking for a mother for Meggie?"

"I told you the truth. Meggie doesn't need a mother, but she could use a stepmother who loves her."

Azure still had her arms around his awaist and squeezed him tight. "If that's a proposal I'll think about it. In the meantime, if you want to make me happy, kiss me again."

"What about your cousin?"

"Thawe is a big boy, he's seen people kiss," she said against his lips.

"But . . ."

"He's taking poor old Raffles for a walk to escape either his father or my mother." She bit his lower lip. "Right now all Thawe cares about is getting away from them."

"They're here?"

"I saw the headlights through the window when they turned off the road. That's why I dragged you out here. Now shut up and kiss me before my cousin shows up and stops all our fun."

"We wouldn't want that now, would we?"

Her bright smile rivaled the sparkling snow around them.

"I need one more kiss before we go back and face the music. Oh, and before I forget to mention it, I love you too." Her words were the sweetest words of love he had ever heard. "Now shut up and kiss me."

===#==#===

Dear Reader,

Thank you for reading *Christmas Lights*. Although Brownville Junction and the Brown property is fictional, the area of Maine where it is located in beautiful and well worth a visit.

Several locations in New York are real, but as an author tends to do, I have taken liberties with them.

I have tried to make it as error free as possible, but if you find boo-boos in the book please feel free to let me know.

Whether you read this in December or July, I hope all your holidays bring you joy.

I hope you have enjoyed *Christmas Lights*.

Love,

Liberty Blake

About the Author

Liberty Blake lives in New England in a large communal home with several of her children and five grandchildren, four dogs, and five cats. It is a wonderfully hectic family home.

Liberty began writing stories on a toy typewriter that was replaced with a real typewriter when she was nine. She has slowed down at times, but she has never stopped writing.

Liberty loves traveling, long walks on the beach, and looking at handsome men.

Visit Liberty's Spellroom on blogspot or send a friend request on Facebook.

The Counterfeit Bride
(Boundless Billionaires)
By Liberty Blake

Texas rancher and bar owner Cassidy Flynn is shocked to learn the bride's name in an upcoming high society wedding – Cassiopeia Dolmides. Cassidy is a woman of secrets; the deepest is the identity she was born with and thought she had escaped long ago. If this bride is impersonating Cassidy, what trouble will that cause Cassidy and her infant son?

Greek tycoon Theron Christofides needs to gain possession of Dolmides Cruise Lines and the little Greek island where it left a shipwrecked eyesore. A lot of people are at risk without his intervention. Old man Dolmides will sell on one condition: Theron must marry Dolmides' illegitimate daughter. Seeing no other way to rescue the island's people, Theron agrees to sacrifice himself and his future.

As Theron stands at the altar with his bride-to-be, a fiery-haired woman in snakeskin boots and a cowboy hat interrupts their vows by calling his bride a fraud. In order for the wedding to continue, Theron must convince Cassidy Flynn to drop her lawsuit. Can he withstand Cassidy's allure while he gains her cooperation? Or will they both be consumed by the fire of desire?

Praise for Liberty Blake's
The Counterfeit Bride

On my vacation I was able to read The Counterfeit Bride and LOVED it! Can't wait to read some more! (Kathleen Brooks, author of the Bluegrass series.)

I loved The Counterfeit Bride. Liberty Blake really made that little Texas girl come alive. (Patricia Grasso, author of To Charm a Prince.)

This book is awesome, amazing!!! If you love sexy, gorgeous, hot, billionaires, LIBERTY BLAKE is the new queen of romance!!!! I can't remember the last time I read such a fab love story!!! (Heather Peters, author of The Rules of the Game series.)

Looking for your next great read? A case of mistaken identity and enough sparks to light up the skies on the Fourth of July make for one exciting story!!! Liberty Blake pulls you in and keeps you hooked throughout! (Angelique Miller)

The Misplaced Bride
(Boundless Billionaires)
By
Liberty Blake

Ajax Pappas had watched his friend Theron Christofides squirm in front of the altar with a combination of mirth and pity. Just a few short weeks later Ajax is called to his father's side where he learns his father is very sick.

His father's one desire is to see Ajax settled down and married in the Greek tradition. In order to avoid his mother's matchmaking, Ajax must produce His Misplaced Bride.

(Coming soon!)

48908189R00124

Made in the USA
Middletown, DE
01 October 2017